PRAISE AND AWARDS FOR *THE LAND*

ADVENTURES IN YELL

"Entertaining, thought-provoking and educational, the EcoSeekers' debut, *The Land of Curiosities,* is a revelation for kids and parents alike. This series is sure to help readers appreciate the history of the conservation movement in America, and to inspire them to do all they can to preserve and protect our natural environment today."
Dick Durbin
U.S. Senator (D-IL)

"I look forward to sharing *The Land of Curiosities* with my own children so they may learn powerful lessons in environmental history through this entertaining and thought-provoking story. The EcoSeekers' first book is a great achievement."
Robert F. Kennedy, Jr.

"EcoSeekers is an innovative and fun approach to showing the power and joy of environmentalism. While taking us on a journey through history, *The Land of Curiosities* tells us much about the challenges we face today. The investment you make in buying this book will return interest to the planet for generations to come."
Frances Beinecke
President, Natural Resources Defense Council

"With good story telling, compelling characters, unusual natural wonders and intriguing wild creatures, this series will fascinate young readers while letting them thoughtfully consider past and current debates about how people interact with nature and wildlife."
Larry Schweiger
President and CEO, National Wildlife Federation

"This book reminded me of all the books I loved so much as a kid. Just wish it had been in print back then! Once it's published, I'll buy a dozen copies to give to the budding conservationists I know."
Martha Marks
Co-Founder & President, Republicans for Environmental Protection

"Young readers will delight in *The Land of Curiosities.* This is the first in a series that introduces important historical events through courageous young characters, and highlights the importance of conserving our environment. A wonderful book for children and parents to read together."
NELL NEWMAN
Co-Founder and President of Newman's Own Organics

"This creative story will inspire the next generation of stewards for the environment and engage its readers in an understanding that something bigger than the human experience operates in the world. A most needed tool for a sustainable future."
REV. SALLY G. BINGHAM
Environmental Minister for the Diocese of California & President of the Regeneration Project / Interfaith Power and Light

"Young readers will identify in their hearts and minds with the vividly human actors in this compelling drama, set in a fascinating place in time and space. Through natural sympathy, they will absorb the important environmental and spiritual lessons of this well-written and entertaining book."
RABBI RACHEL COWAN
Director, The Institute for Jewish Spirituality

"I was excited to see that the EcoSeekers included the role of religion and personal faith in defining America's land ethic in a way that is enjoyable and accessible for young adults."
PETER ILLYN
Restoring Eden / Christians for Environmental Stewardship

"A look at the country's first national park through the eyes of young adventurers will appeal to those who want to learn more about Yellowstone and its mysteries."
PHYLLIS SMITH
Author, Bozeman and the Gallatin Valley

"This page-turning adventure has all the makings of a roller coaster ride through history – that it also delves into important environmental and social issues means it is not just a great read but a book young people should read, a combination rarely achieved."
TODD PAGLIA
Executive Director, ForestEthics

"*The Land of Curiosities* offers one of the most complete pictures of the history of the destruction of the bison and the degradation of the natural resources of America I have read to date. The book does a wonderful job of illustrating the importance of conservation and protection of the resources of the natural world. This book is enlightening to not only the targeted audience of children but to adults as well."
JIM STONE
Executive Director, Intertribal Bison Cooperative

"This engaging book vividly brings to life America's wild west through wonderfully crafted adventures of discovery. It promises to both educate and entertain, and delivers a powerful message about the importance of worldwide conservation."
TAMAR DATAN
Executive Vice President, Amazon Conservation Team

MOONBEAM CHILDREN'S BOOK AWARD
Best First Book (GOLD), Pre-Teen Fiction-Intermediate/Middle Grade (SILVER)

BENJAMIN FRANKLIN BOOK AWARD
Best First Book (SILVER)

Additional awards include **NAUTILUS BOOK AWARD** (GOLD), and **MOM'S CHOICE AWARDS®** (SILVER) for best juvenile and young adult historical fiction.

2nd Edition Published by The EcoSeekers™

First edition Published 2007

For further information please contact:
The EcoSeekers
48 South Broadway, P.O. Box 637
Nyack, NY 10960.

Art direction and book design by Paula Winicur
Interior illustrations by David Erickson
Cover illustration by Tom Newsom
Map illustration by David Lowe

10 9 8 7 6 5 4 3 2 1

The text of this book is set in Parango, Block Berthold Condensed, Voluta, and Triplex.
Manufactured and printed in the United States of America.

This book is printed on FSC-certified, 30% post-consumer recycled paper, using soy-based ink.

The EcoSeekers is a proud member of the Green Press Initiative.

Written by
DEANNA NEIL

Conceived and produced by
DAVID NEIL

James, Mattie, and Alice Clifton

AGED 12 YEARS, 30 YEARS, AND 9 YEARS

Table of Contents

GUY HOUSE

Chapter 1
THE WEST

James was told that it would be a town, but as the horses clopped forward, he knew right away that Bozeman, Montana, was different from any town back East where he grew up. Main Street was nothing more than a wide muddy path with rows of wagon trains parked on the side. About a dozen dusty general stores and trade shops peeked out from behind the wagons. There was a flagpole. There was a flag. That was it.

James arrived with his sister, Alice, and his mother, Mattie, on a brisk Tuesday morning. They stepped out onto the muddy street and breathed in the strangely dry air. Beyond the small town, fields of vibrant flowers spread out in every direction. In the distance, the mountains stood watching over the town like silent sentinels. Men with long, bushy moustaches and sweaty armpits leaned against the building posts. Their faces looked like masks leathered by the sun and dirt. As James walked past, the men stared at him with gleaming eyes above their dirty cheeks.

"C'mere, boy," one man said. "What's that list for?"

"It's for supplies, sir," James replied, trying to keep his distance.

"Give it here."

The man looked over the supply list and grunted.

"You headin' up to Annis and Cooper? You takin' a wagon out?"

"No, sir. We're meeting up with Reverend Lawson here."

"Ah, the fine preacher. Nothin' but heathens for him out in these parts. You won't find much religion out here, just a bunch of boys drinkin' and minin' and tryin' to make a dollar." James looked back at his mother Mattie and his sister Alice, who was clutching her Bible.

"You must be the Clifton boy," the man finally said, smiling and revealing a set of yellow, stained teeth.

"Yes, sir. How did you know?"

"Well, James Clifton, that's my job—to pay attention. Plus, we don't get many people who plan on stickin' around here for very long. We'll see if you make it."

James lifted his head. *Of course I can make it,* he thought, as he confronted the man with his gaze.

"It seems to me that you have too nice of a face to be a boy from out West," the man said. James clenched his fists. More than anything he hated being told he was handsome. He thought handsome men were boring and simpleminded and only got by on their looks. James wanted to make a difference in the world, as his father had. Instead, people were always commenting on his "lovely" sandy brown hair, his "dreamy" hazel eyes and how his cheeks "simply glowed" after he came in from playing ball. He had played rough at sports in New York, in the hopes that his nose would be broken, shattering his looks forever. Clearly, that hadn't worked.

"You stayin' at the Guy House?" the man asked. James nodded. The Guy House was the hotel on the northwest corner of Main and Black Streets. Mattie said that's where they would stay for the next few weeks while they built a house. The going rate was two dollars a night.

"You with this wagon train here?" the man asked, pointing to the row of horse-drawn, misshapen carts on wheels.

James nodded again. He saw his mother and Alice talking to some local folk who had come out to greet them. They were pointing out the different stores and shops. Alice coughed into her handkerchief, which reminded him to pick up Epsom salts and peppermint.

"Say, you didn't see a rough lookin' fellow and a red haired boy on your trip, did you? I've been keepin' a watch out," said the man.

"No, I don't reckon' so," James said, shaking his head. The man seemed wary of the aforementioned travelers. James looked around anxiously for a moment.

"Where you comin' from?" the man asked, quickly changing the subject.

"New York, sir."

"That's pretty far. We've got people here from all over though, not just the rough boys. Industrious folk. A share of farmers from around the Midwestern parts pickin' up their farmin', some folks from the South. Lots of people ran away from the war, you know, come out to a territory to get out of the states entirely. Not that a young'n like you knows about the war anyway."

James wasn't stupid. He knew about the war between the Northern and Southern states, and he knew about the lives that were lost. He clenched his fists again, but quickly put them behind his back to hide his disrespect.

"Although it's tough out here," the man went on. "After all that time out in the wilderness, livin' in tents for battle, shootin' people, tryin' to make do, you'd think that people would have had enough. They'd just want a bit of civilization. But some folks have a sense for adventure and new beginnings."

He looked intensely at James. "Was your father in the war?"

"Yes, he was, sir."

"He's not over at Fort Ellis now, is he?"

"No. He's not." It was quiet for a moment.

"How was your journey out here?"

"Just fine, sir."

But it hadn't been fine at all. There was dust everywhere, and the days seemed never-ending. When they passed by rivers, the mosquitoes half ate him up. He could hear his mother's muffled crying sometimes at night, even over the coyotes hollering. James just pulled the featherbed up over his head.

His father would have taken care of her. His father wouldn't have made them travel across the whole country. That was the doing of the puffy-cheeked Reverend Lawson—Mother's new husband. *The preacher doesn't even know our family well enough to take care of us proper. He married Mother then left for Montana two years ago,* James mulled.

He remembered the family meeting his mother called: "It's been some time since your father's death. We need to look forward to the future. It's not right for you to be raised without a father," Mattie had said, sounding more like she was convincing herself. "I am going to be married to a kind man from the church. You will meet him tomorrow before he leaves. He'll be circuit riding out West and when things settle down we'll go to be with him. It is all arranged. Do you understand?"

James snapped back into his conversation with the man.

"From what I understand, most people consider the trip out here pretty miserable. You must have been lucky. But by the looks of you, and from what little I know about the preacher, you prob'ly traveled by rail for some of the way," the man said.

It was true. The trip wasn't always bad. The train ride was fun—James enjoyed looking out over the wide, rolling country. He had opened the window to stick his head out and let his hair dance in the wind. Sometimes the air was so powerful coming at him that he had to turn sideways to breathe. He loved the railroads and their power. It always amazed him that humans could create something so tremendous and useful.

Outside the train buffalo roamed as far as the eye could see. Even with the sounds of the train lurching along, he could hear the herds pounding the earth like thunder. CLANG! James would hear from a window nearby. Some people hunted the buffalo out the windows for sport, but his mother wouldn't let him. Alice went to pieces anytime she heard the shots. She thought the buffalo were the most beautiful things she had ever seen. Alice couldn't stand the idea that people would shoot the animals just for fun.

Alice had her father's olive complexion and wavy dark hair. Her bangs added to the impression that she was bouncing, almost skipping, when she walked. Back at home in New York, James would see her coming through the crowded streets, bobbing up and down in the distance. But recently she seemed more frail and pale than usual, and her eyes looked red around the rims. When Alice coughed, her shoulders shook violently.

"Jamesie, Jamesie," she bobbed toward him from a distance, singing to herself. The man looked down and saw she was carrying a Bible. For a second, James had the feeling the man might try to steal it from her.

"She's trying to practice for the preacher. She even marked all the places that mention animals and nature just to share with him," James explained. Miles grunted.

"Well, sir, I have to be on my way," James said to the man. But just as he turned to leave, his eye caught sight of a newspaper article posted in the window. He took a closer look.

"That article was fresh printed last week," the man said proudly. "Our first edition of the newspaper."

THE AVANT COURIER

BOZEMAN, MONTANA TERRITORY — SEPTEMBER 13, 1871

EASTERN MONTANA, signally favored by a fine salubrious climate—her wonderful geysers; the falls of the Yellowstone, the most marvelous in the world; the numerous mineral springs, possessing medicinal virtues of a remarkable character, as proven by the experience of a number of afflicted persons restored to health quite recently; is destined to be a great public resort, equaling anything of the kind ever known. The advent of the Northern Pacific will bring in the tide.

James looked at the date: September 13, 1871. He didn't understand everything the article said: What was "salubrious"? What was "the advent"? They would be "bringing a tide" into the middle of the country? But he was pretty sure that an afflicted person was a sick person, and that this place—Yellowstone—could help a sick person.

"Are the medical. . .medicinal. . .er. . .mineral springs near by?" James asked.

"They're a few sleeps away from Bozeman on horseback. There ain't no trails out there—just wilderness—so there's no wagons other than the one or two that carry your supplies. I know grown men who lost their way and nearly starved out there." The man bent around the doorframe. "Here, take the article," he said, peeling the newsprint from the window with his ink-stained fingers.

"Are you sure it's okay to do that, sir?"

"Of course I am. I work here." He puffed out his chest a bit. "I'm a newspaperman. Name is Miles. Dr. Wright runs the paper, but I do a fair share of reporting. Well, so far. We just started up a couple of weeks ago."

James was surprised. Miles didn't look like a newspaperman, except for the smudges on his hands. The newspapermen from back East were always ruddy-cheeked and overeager, with little pencils stuck behind their ears. He remembered when they came to the house after his father was killed. They asked all sorts of serious questions, and James didn't really understand what was going on. He was only about four or five at the time and had peeked out from behind his mother's black mourning skirt as the reporters shot out questions. The incident took place years ago, but he could easily remember every minute.

"Mrs. Clifton, please tell us more about your

husband," they asked with their pencils perched, ready to write his mother's every word.

"My husband died for our country. He is now in heaven with the many other brave men who died fighting to save the Union and to free the slaves. He was a proud abolitionist, strongly influenced by the anti-slavery teachings of our Quaker neighbors."

The newspapermen scribbled furiously onto their notepads. They barely noticed the passion and pain in his mother's voice.

This newspaperman, Miles, was leaning against a post and spitting. No, James didn't think he looked like those New York reporters at all. He looked like he wanted to eat James, not talk to him. For some reason, James found him oddly appealing. *I bet he knows things about people,* he thought admiringly. James had a practical nature, so newspapers had always interested him. Those New York reporters weren't so enchanting to James—but Miles had a way about him that James liked. James flinched when the gruff reporter started talking again.

"Listen, Clifton boy, once you get your bearings, if you need anything, you just call on me—Miles." He handed James back his supplies list. "I've got a sense that you'll be havin' questions of your own soon enough, especially if you read the rest of that there article. You can find most of what you're lookin' for inside my shop here. You can get the rest at the blacksmith across the street." James peered around Miles' shoulder and saw a foyer with all sorts of goods: axes, plows, wheels. There were a few little trinkets as well: music boxes, old recipe books, a deck of cards.

"I know my shop ain't much to boast about, but it pays the bills while I try to make this newspaper work. We all have to make compromises. Most folks around here work lots of trades at the same time, anyhow."

"Thank you. Maybe we'll go across the street first," James said, tentatively.

"Suit yourself." Miles bowed when Alice approached, then turned on his boot and went inside. *Maybe this man isn't so intimidating after all,* thought James.

"James! Look at all these purple flowers I found. Aren't they pretty? Who was that scary-looking man?" Alice asked.

"Nobody. C'mon." James stuffed the article and his list back into his pocket, and they crossed the street to start gathering supplies.

Twilight hit the clouds with an angry pink, then submitted to the calming darkness. Settled into the hotel for the night, James glanced over at his sister's sleeping face illuminated by the soft glow of the kerosene lamp.

"Mother?" James asked tentatively.

"Yes?"

"I found this article in town today. I remember how you once took the waters in Saratoga... I was thinking that maybe it would be good for Alice."

He reached into his pocket and handed her Miles' article. Mattie gave him an encouraging nod, and started reading it out loud, mumbling, "Gentlemen who have just returned from the volcano region of the Yellowstone country report that the statements heretofore made regarding the wonders there exhibited are in no ways exaggerated...."

"No, that's not the right part. Look what it says at the end," James said. "The rather pleasant part about the healing waters."

"Oh, I see," Mattie said, reading on. "You want to

take your sister there to the hot springs so that her cough gets better?"

James nodded, and his mother smiled at him.

"James, you're very protective. I think it's your father in you." She ran her fingers through his hair and then kissed him on the forehead. James could barely recall what his father looked like, let alone remember his attributes. But Mattie told so many stories about his father that James felt like he could picture him; Mattie's memories became James' as well. *It's funny how after I hear a story so often, I can feel like I was actually there,* James thought.

Mattie took the article and put it in her skirt pocket. "Jed should be down from Helena any day now. We'll

discuss it with him when he arrives. Say your prayers and get in bed."

James was upset with himself for not guarding the words closer. Maybe Reverend Lawson wouldn't approve at all. As he lay in bed, the words from the article circled in his mind: *What were the wonders? Who were the gentlemen who went? What did a volcano look like? What else was so mysterious about this Yellowstone?*

That night, James dreamt of his father. They sat together in a Civil War dog tent and cannonballs dropped all around them. Screams rang outside, painful sounds of men dying, but he and his father just sat in the tent playing a game of cards. Every once in a while a person or object would fly against the tent making it shake, but neither of them seemed to mind. When James won the round of cards, his father reached into his pocket and pulled out a tiny shovel.

"Let's see what you can do with this," he said.

James took the tiny shovel and started digging. He hit a hot pool of steaming water.

"Look, Father! It's the healing water!" James said.

James reached inside the water and felt a tiny object.

He carefully pulled it out and saw that it was a miniature, living buffalo. To his surprise, the buffalo turned to James and started talking. "Where are all of your friends, James?" The animal said in Alice's voice. James dropped the animal and it went scampering off outside into the battlefield. He turned back to his father, who had vanished.

"Father?" James was calling. But there was no answer. He was alone in the tent.

James woke up sweating. When he realized where he was, his heart ached. James felt no sense of belonging out here. "Where are all of my friends?" he whispered to himself. He missed the real towns from home. He felt alone and somehow responsible for his mother and Alice, despite the Reverend's anticipated arrival. Would he ever overcome that lonesome feeling that had shadowed him from east to west? James felt like those solitary tumbleweeds along the wagon trail rolling off into nowhere.

"Father, if you're listening, I want you to know that

I will do anything I can to protect Mother and Alice. I hope that I can make a home for us out here." The words scared him, but James knew that saying them out loud would help him to be strong.

A lone wolf howled, and there were sounds of men getting drunk down the street at the Chesnut Saloon. James fell into the darkness of sleep.

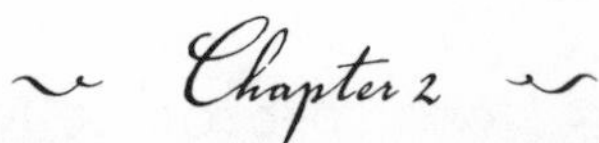

THE TERRIBLE GIFT INCIDENT

Mattie sat on a three-legged stool by the window of their room at the Guy House and looked up from her sewing almost every hour.

"The letter said he was coming *tomorrow,*" Alice reminded her mother. She and James looked at each other and rolled their eyes.

They had been in town for a few days anticipating Reverend Lawson's arrival. Mattie had bought some calico and cut out a new bonnet. Her hair was tied up as usual, in an elaborately pinned bun at the back of her head. Her form-fitting dress had tiny buttons from the hem to the neck and along each sleeve. A bustle jutted out of the back of her dress, and the fabric skirted the ground as she walked. She spent the whole evening fussing about clothes and sending James and Alice around town for final errands.

At the break of dawn, Mattie gently woke James and Alice. "It's time to get ready," she said.

"I wonder if she slept at all," James said to Alice as he groaned and got out of bed. Mattie put Alice in a white dress with a purple sash around the back and James in trousers, shined shoes and a small bowtie around his neck. She slicked back his hair. He was rather uncomfortable as he stepped outside into the morning sunlight.

There weren't many families in the area yet, but James was relieved to see a few young faces accompanying their parents in town as they went about their business. They eyed each other curiously. Folks lingered on Main Street to greet Reverend Lawson and the incoming party.

"Hello, I am Mrs. Blakely," said a friendly-looking woman in a colorful bonnet. "You can just call me Henrietta." She laughed shrilly. "And this is my son, Tom." She pulled up her collar to shield herself from the biting wind.

"It feels like winter is approaching all too fast,"

she babbled on. "But the weather out here is so fickle. One minute it's hailing, the next minute it'll be sunny. Storms come and go within minutes, it seems. The weather just can't seem to make up its mind! And who is this mighty handsome young man?"

James cringed. "This is my son, James," Mattie said with a smile.

"Nice to meet you, ma'am." James mustered up his polite manners.

"You should call on us for dinner one night this week. We'll make a special turkey stew with peas," Henrietta said. Mattie blushed and accepted. James felt nauseous at the idea of turkey stew with peas. He looked over at Tom, whose teeth were chattering. James thought he heard him mumble, "Tastes like vomit," but he wasn't certain.

Tom had stick-straight black hair and a pale face that carried little expression. "Do you like to ice skate?" Tom asked, clearly this time, shivering all the while. His voice was flat and, for all the exaggerated animation of his mother, Tom had none. James couldn't tell if Tom's question about ice skating was an insult or an invitation.

"Sure," James answered wearily. He figured it was

the safe answer.

"The McDonald boys and I go on the frozen stream," Tom said. "You should come with us once it's solid. Sometimes we go icicle hunting too. Whoever finds the most curious looking icicle or ice patch wins. I usually find it." James was relieved to discover

that this was an invitation, after all. Then he cast his eyes down in disappointment.

"I don't know if we'll be staying through the winter. It depends on the preacher."

"Do you always call him the preacher? Isn't he your father?" Tom asked bluntly.

"He's...well, sort of...in a manner. He's my stepfather."

"Oh," Tom stated flatly.

"His real name is Jedediah Lawson," James answered, embarrassed.

"Sure, I know his name," Tom said. "He's been through town lots of times."

Tom's mother chimed in. "Well, it was very nice meeting you. We're going to run some errands at the creamery and warm up inside for a bit until *the preacher* arrives." She looked at James, then laughed wildly, hitting Mattie on the arm and throwing her head back like a strange clucking chicken.

She sighed as her laughter subsided. "Don't worry, dear. They'll call him Jed soon enough," she said, wiping the laugh-tears away from the corners of her eyes. James turned red.

"Good day," Mattie replied quickly. James bid farewell as Mrs. Blakely enthusiastically ushered Tom away. Tom just lifted his hand stiffly and shuffled along.

"I think I see him," James said to his mother, pointing to the distance behind Tom's head. Immediately, other people started craning their necks and pointing.

Reverend Lawson hadn't come in from Helena alone. A party of horsemen and wagons appeared in the distance and slowly made their way toward town. They looked like a tiny swarm of insects at first, but they slowly separated into individuals as they got closer. James shifted his eyes from the party to the mountains, and he suddenly noticed how glorious the scenery was. The town of Bozeman was surrounded by grey, jagged triangles tipped with white. The sky was so enormous and blue that it looked flat. James took a deep breath and felt drawn to the adventures that lay beyond those peaks. *What were the mountains hiding?* he wondered.

James' eyes watered from the bright, cold forenoon. When he lowered his gaze back down, the new arrivals had made significant progress and were at the very edge of Bozeman. They had a mule train with them carrying covered wagons with supplies for the town. Shopkeepers emerged and warmly greeted Reverend Lawson as they examined their new shipment of goods. Mr. and Mrs. Story approached, along with John and Sophia Guy who ran the Guy House. Sam Lewis, the black barber and property owner, greeted the preacher with a friendly hello. Of course, Miles came out to shake Reverend Lawson's hand and get some lofty words for the newspaper.

Reverend Lawson had come down from Helena where he had been circuit-riding, touring around the West and delivering religious teachings. It was strange for James to see a preacher in everyday clothing. He

had on an old brown jacket, and his collared shirt was stained. He wore a waistcoat, which looked kind of like a vest. Almost all of the men wore waistcoats and differently shaped felt hats. The preacher had very thin lips and eyebrows. James thought he looked different from when they met a few years ago in New York.

Other than the preacher, the rest of the party from Helena consisted of rough and grizzled men, mostly coming down from the mines. They all had that same glowering look as Miles, the whites of their eyes standing out against their sun-scarred skin. There were a few Chinese that were passing through en route to Virginia City. Lots of Chinese people worked on the railroads and in the mines.

James noticed a boy about his age handling whiskey crates near the saloon with a man who must have been the boy's father. The boy had dark red hair and a scar on his upper lip. The man wore a long black coat and gloves without fingertips.

They worked silently together, passing along crates of whiskey, removing saddles and lifting up the horses' hooves to see what kind of damage was done on the journey. James felt the need to watch them, as if at any moment they might pounce on the innocent townspeople like panthers.

"It's not polite to stare, James," his mother said and pinched his arm. The preacher made his way over to James, Alice, and Mattie. He gave Mattie a kiss on the cheek.

"James, good to see you, son." He walked over and shook James' hand. After all her talking, James had expected Alice to throw her arms around the preacher, but she stood very quiet and shy.

"Hello, little one," he said.

"I'm not little," she stated.

"Alice!" Mattie started in with a chastising tone.

"That's fine, we're all created in different shapes and sizes. And you are neither big nor small. You are just perfect." Alice smiled and gave him a hug.

"There's my Alice," the preacher said. "Oh, and I have something for you." Alice's face lit up as Reverend Lawson went to the back of a wagon. Alice spotted some animal fuzz sticking out from his arms. She grabbed James' arm in excitement. It had to be a new pet! She loved pets. The preacher got her a white bunny one year for Christmas and James never heard the end of it. It was always, "Bunny said this, Bunny did that." She claimed her bunny spoke to her. She said he was related to the white rabbit that was always late in *Alice in Wonderland,* that this bunny was his British cousin and always on time.

The preacher turned around and knelt down to her, but instead of a new pet, he unfolded a small pile of fur pelts.

"This here is coyote," he displayed it for her with a smile on his face. "I traded with some Crow Indians for it. And this one here is beaver pelt. Feel how soft." But Alice didn't budge at all. She stood there as stiff as a tree trunk. James saw her lip start quivering and little tears pooling in her eyes.

"Don't you want to touch it? Don't be afraid; it's dead. It's not going to hurt you," the preacher said, misreading Alice's reason for being upset. Mattie quickly interjected herself into the conversation.

"That was so kind of you, Jed. They are beautiful," she said.

"But I didn't even get to show her the most beautiful one yet. Look at this!" And with that, he unfolded a buffalo robe. It will keep you warm, that's for sure," the preacher said. "Especially on a day like today."

"That's real nice of you... sir. Wow, it really is soft," James said awkwardly as he outstretched his arm to take the robe and cover up Alice's deep frown.

"Well, it's my pleasure. And don't worry, son, I've got something really special for you," Reverend Lawson said as he turned around and started rummaging in the wagon. James saw this as a chance to take Alice away before she caused trouble.

"I just realized that I left my gift for *you* back at home!" James said with more force than was necessary. "C'mon Alice, let's go get it," James grabbed his sister by the hand, but she didn't budge.

"Why, James, that was so thoughtful of you. But son, that's okay. You can get it later," the preacher began.

At this moment, Alice burst into tears and screamed, "HE KILLED THEM!"

Reverend Lawson stopped rummaging through his strongbox in the back of the wagon. A few towns-people stopped talking and curiously looked on from behind wagons. James thought he saw some people peek out of their windows too.

James had never seen the preacher get angry and

wasn't sure that he really wanted to. Reverend Lawson turned to Mattie.

"Everything okay with the little one?" he asked nervously.

"I AM NOT A LITTLE ONE!" Alice shouted. The preacher jumped back with surprise at her force. He looked around and shrugged, smiling timidly to the onlookers.

James knew that trouble was brewing.

"Alice, you've got to get control of yourself!" Mattie instructed. "I'm so sorry, Jed; she has a strange connection to animals."

"LOOK, YOU CAN SEE THE HOLES IN THE FURS WHERE THEY WERE MURDERED."

"Alice. . .stop shouting," James said through clenched teeth. The man in the black coat and the red-headed boy had made their way over toward them to investigate what was happening. The man's cracked and bloody knuckles poked through his fingerless gloves and rested on his gun. James caught his eye and then quickly looked away.

The preacher stood dumbfounded at the whole situation. This was not the greeting that he had expected. He looked over at Mattie, hoping for guidance. James thought the preacher turned a pinkish shade.

"Mattie, I hope you've taught your children the practicalities of life. We can't have them fantasizing about fairies and talking beasts forever," the preacher finally said. James didn't like how he was talking to his mother, but he wanted Alice to stop making a scene. Most of the other people had turned away, but the man in the black coat and the red-headed boy still lurked.

"Be reasonable, Alice. These will keep us warm in the winter," James said, trying to settle everything before the two got any closer or heard any more of their business.

"No. Maybe the buffalo one, but the other two are just decorations. They're not even shaped like anything. And the coyote still has a head on it," she lamented, her voice getting high-pitched. She coughed a few times in between her tears.

James looked at the fur and noticed the little slits where the eyes used to be. For a brief moment, he was also disgusted.

"Alice, it is very rude of you to insult Jed after he provided such generous gifts," Mattie reprimanded. But Alice wouldn't stop. She started rifling through her Bible to find one of her marked pages about animals.

" 'But ask now the beasts, and they shall teach thee; the fowls of the air, and they shall tell thee: Or speak to the earth, and it shall teach thee: and the fishes of the sea shall declare unto thee. . .' ."

"Alice, stop," James interrupted.

But she continued by speaking even louder, her finger following every line.

"James, take your sister back to the hotel right now," Mattie said sharply. "She is not to come out until she comes to her senses. Jed will give you your gift later. Alice, we'll discuss this incident later this evening. It was mighty inappropriate for you to cause such a stir."

The color receded from the preacher's face, and he returned to his normal doughy-colored flesh. "That's right, son. We'll exchange our gifts later. Take these with you so that your sister gets used to them," he said, trying to laugh and keep the situation light-hearted. "I tell you, at least she knows her Bible!"

This is just fine, James thought angrily, *how am I going to get him a gift? I don't have any money.*

Chapter 3

BLOODY KNUCKLES

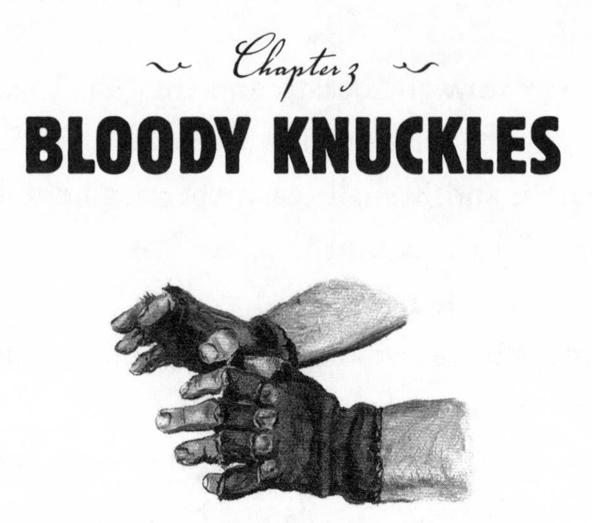

James and Alice walked hastily down the wooden porches of Main Street back to the hotel. James could feel the eyes of the red-haired boy searing into his back as they walked away. Something about that boy and his father made the hairs on James' arms stand on end. He encouraged Alice to move faster.

"Alice, look. They're dead," he said holding up the furs. "We see dead animals all the time. We eat them, we hunt them, and we need them to live. You have to stop acting like this; you're being peculiar," James said.

"You're peculiar for thinking it's okay to kill them. Everyone else is peculiar but me."

"Alice, that doesn't make sense. If you were the

only normal one and everyone else was peculiar, it still means that you're the only one who's different—which makes you peculiar," James said. But she wasn't listening to his arguments.

"But we don't need them. I already have furs. We're plenty warm," she insisted. "I wanted a live animal, not a dead one. I don't care for the West at all. It's terrible and unpleasant. All anybody does is shoot things."

"Alice, we shot things in New York too," James reasoned.

"Where are we goin' in such a rush?" a voice said from inside a doorway. James stopped. It was Miles again. He put his forearm up against the doorframe, leaned casually, then spit.

"Those are some nice furs you've got there," he said. "Won't they come in handy in a month or two!"

James was struck with an idea.

"What could I get in trade for these two pelts?" he asked and raised up the beaver and coyote skins. He would have to keep the buffalo one, or else the preacher and his mother would notice the furs were all gone. Plus, he thought it was a really nice robe.

"Oh, quite a bit. What sort of thing you looking for? "

"Something a preacher would want."

"I see, a welcoming gift. That's very thoughtful of you, boy," Miles said in his raspy voice. He displayed his yellow teeth again. "Why don't you come in? I've got a few things in here that might do."

James tentatively walked inside the door, tugging Alice by the hand to follow. As they walked into the foyer, James noticed a narrow staircase up the back. He heard men's voices upstairs.

"You just tell me if you see anything out here that might interest you," Miles said. He rubbed the stubble on his face with his hand.

"Miles!" a deep male voice called from up the stairs.

"I'll be back right soon," he said. He turned on his heel and walked up the stairs. James put the furs on the wooden table in the corner and sat his sister down. He hoped that Miles wouldn't write about his sister's fit in the paper.

"A woman running for president! Well, she is just ridiculous," he heard one voice boom from upstairs. There was quiet and then loud laughter. James was glad that his mother wasn't there. She was sympathetic to the suffragists, the people who believed that women should be able to vote.

"It seems to me that the railroads are the only answer for us to make money out here. They've got to be coming soon. Look how many men they sent out this year alone to evaluate the line."

"We really needed your Harvard University degree to tell us that."

James caught little snippets of the men's conversation as he walked around the room. Alice just sat in her chair swinging her legs. She seemed to be over her tantrum, but she buried her head in her Bible looking for more passages to recite to the preacher.

"It's the scientists that are doing these expeditions into Yellowstone. They're interested in the curiosities just as much as we all are. The government sends them out. General Grant sees the potential," he heard another voice say. James had learned about President Ulysses S. Grant in school back East. Grant became a general in the Civil War. Sometimes people called him General Grant; sometimes they called him President Grant. He was both.

"If they had their way, they'd chop up all the oddities and take them back to a museum back East. I heard someone was even taking Indian skulls."

James walked by a doll, and then passed by an old,

broken clock. He saw a whole pile of guns in a wooden crate.

"If you could have heard Jim Bridger talk about that place. . .I had the honor of shaking his hand and he said that he saw Satan himself."

"Spinning yarns! Spinning yarns!" they all huffed. James heard a thump, like someone slamming his fist on the table.

"Unreliable fur traders can't tell a story right. They sit around campfires and entertain themselves with hot air. I bet only a fraction of their stories are true."

James wanted to hear more, so he inched his way toward the stairs.

"Alice, stay here for a minute," James said quietly.

She didn't look up from reading. "Okay," she said with ease.

James slowly crept up the wooden stairs on his tiptoes. A shaft of light came through the windows to illuminate tiny dust particles floating in the air.

"I hear there's still gold to be found out there."

"Alder's Gulch is tapped. You wouldn't find anything over there."

"Farther out I bet you could."

"We should start putting down property there.

Ranches."

James thought it was funny how they were called ranches out West. Back East they were just called farms. There was no real difference other than the name, as far as he could tell.

"You can't grow anything out there."

"The Bottler brothers are doing well. I hear that McCartney's got a hotel by the hot springs and that quite a fair share of people pass through. Some folks on the expeditions as well—the fancy photographers and all."

A hotel! James thought. *That's where we can stay when we go down to the springs for Alice.*

When he came to the second level of Miles' shop, James poked his head around the corner. There was a collection of printing machinery and a group of men sitting around a table smoking tobacco. Smoke from their pipes slowly floated around their faces. Some of them had their feet propped up on the table. One man was playing darts. The table behind them was covered with papers. James spotted a telegraph in the corner.

"Did you see Billy Knuckles and his boy, Red?" one of the men asked.

"I think you mean *Bloody* Knuckles." They all laughed heartily.

"That poor boy. Even if a man wants to do dirty business, you leave your kids at home."

"There's no home for him to attend, I'm told. Absolutely despicable."

Bloody Knuckles must have been the man in the long coat, James thought.

"I tell you, if I could just set him down and get a few answers out of his trap. . . ." James heard Miles say.

"The days of the vigilantes are over, Miles."

"Not in my book, they're not. I heard he robbed a train just last week."

James had heard all sorts of stories about the vigilantes enforcing law where there were no established rules or any police around to enforce them. The vigilantes would drag prisoners out of jail and hang them without trials. James didn't really know what a trial was, but he knew that not having one was rather bad and unfair.

"I wonder what he wants out there in Yellowstone," Miles said rubbing his stubble again. Then he perked up with a new thought. James saw Miles' boots tapping on the floor.

"The runts are awful quiet down there," he said. James quickly inched his way back downstairs. He could feel his heart pounding.

James was paying so much attention to the voices upstairs that he didn't realize a few of the voices were actually coming from below. He turned and saw Alice surrounded by two figures. They were talking to her in low voices and leaning over her. It was Bloody Knuckles and Red.

"See, I told you James was coming down," Alice said. She jumped up from her chair and ran over to her brother.

"Having a nice conversation upstairs?" the man said as he cracked his neck.

"C-can I help you?" James asked. The man and his son leered for a moment.

"We were just admiring your furs," Bloody Knuckles said. His saliva was thick in his mouth. James looked down at the man's bloody knuckles again. He and Red smelled of sweat and horses. James remembered that they had just arrived from a long journey. Red stared at James with icy blue eyes.

"Unfortunately, gentlemen, these fine furs are now in my possession and not for sale. James and I have just made a trade." Miles came down the stairs, saving the day.

"Is that so?" Bloody Knuckles said.

"Indeed it is," he said. "The name is Miles and you're standin' in my shop."

"Well, it looks like we missed our opportunity, then, didn't we? Come on Red, let's go." Bloody Knuckles made his way to the door.

"You look familiar though, sir. Could I get your name? We like to keep track of all the visitors who come through these parts," Miles said, knowing very well whom he was speaking to.

"We'll only be staying for a sleep or two, no need for introductions," Bloody Knuckles said as they strutted out the door. Once on the porch outside, Bloody Knuckles paused a moment. Then he abruptly turned and pointed a long, mangled finger down at his son.

"You best be watching out for what kind of company you keep," he said to Red instructively. "You should know who your friends are." A chill went down James' spine as he was reminded of his dream.

"Darn, I think I scared him away," Miles said sarcastically. "Where are those nice cigars?" he asked himself and went rummaging through a cabinet behind the store counter.

Then, just below the shelf on the floor, James noticed a small, folded piece of paper. He picked it up and unfolded it carefully. James tried to read it quickly while Miles had his back turned.

Bloody Knuckles, James thought. *The terrible father-son twosome must have dropped it as they were leaving. But who is G and what is the plan?* James stuffed the note into his pocket.

G-
Everything is going according to plan.
BK

"Here they are." Miles found his cigars and opened the box, inhaled and smiled.

"Did you figure on a trade, Clifton?" Miles asked.

James looked down and saw a nice compass in a brass case. The top lifted off, and he could see the compass dial with its spindled lines pointing in all directions.

"I'll take this," James said. It seemed appropriate. Who knew where they would be going when they went out to Yellowstone? He looked down at the compass face and thought of all the different directions that his life could take. What would happen if he went south? North? East? West? He spun it

around and found comfort that the contraption always knew which way was north.

"James?" Alice said.

"What?"

"I don't feel so good." All of her crying and the encounter with the men looked like it had worn her out. Her little dress hung limply on her weary body. She wheezed, and then let out a gurgled sounding cough.

"Okay, let's go."

Chapter 4
SUPPER

At supper that night, everyone sat quietly sipping their soup. No one wanted to rehash the terrible gift incident from earlier in the day. James felt like Bloody Knuckles' letter was burning a hole in his pocket. Should he tell his mother? Was this cause for alarm? Should he tell Miles or the preacher? He started to chew the inside of his lip between soup slurps. At least his silence fit in with the general mood. It was the preacher who finally decided to move the conversation along.

"Well, James. I know you've sacrificed a lot to come out here on this little adventure. So, I wanted to reward you properly with a gift. Please tell me if you are in any way offended by it. Apparently we have not been in each other's company long enough that I recognize your habits," he said as he cleared his throat.

"Yes, sir," James responded. *At least he is trying,* James thought.

The preacher took out a piece of cloth. James unwrapped it but wasn't sure what he was looking at. It looked like a piece of ornate white chalk that had been laminated.

"What is it?" he asked trying not to be disrespectful.

"It's a piece of sinter," Jed said.

"Sinter?" James replied with curiosity.

"It's a souvenir from Yellowstone, around the hot springs—a wonderful curiosity. I'm not sure of how it's made. . .something about the hot waters coming up and depositing little pieces of material, I don't know. I just know it's very rare and extremely difficult to preserve. I had bought you something else, but your mother told me about your noble effort to go take the waters for your sister and your general interest in the place."

James didn't want Alice to know that he thought she was really sick, but he couldn't be annoyed with the preacher because he'd gotten him such a special gift. Alice perked up. "We're going to take the waters?" she asked excitedly. Apparently the reason for going didn't bother her as much as James thought it might.

James looked at his mother in anticipation.

Mattie smiled. "We discussed the article and the possibility of going down to Yellowstone and to the hot springs. We decided that it is a good idea."

"Yippee!" they both cheered. Alice gave James a hug. "This is going to be so much fun. Even more fun than the trip out here!"

James couldn't hide his excitement either. "It'll be the best adventure yet!" he exclaimed.

"But, but, but," Mattie stopped them, "let's not get ahead of ourselves. We need to wait until it warms up a bit. There's no sense in going out now right before winter. We'll stay in town for a few more months and see how Alice does here." James looked over at the preacher wondering why he had agreed to go.

"But what about your work? What about building a house here?" James asked the preacher.

Jed smiled with

his lips closed and said, "I've been touring around this area for a few years now, and I've heard that Yellowstone is the infernal region of the netherworld. There's nothing I'd like more than to look the devil in the eye and preach in his backyard, even if it's just to a small group of adventurers." Jed squinted when he imagined looking the devil in the eye and pointed his finger at an invisible character in his imagination. He took another bite of chicken, put his fork down, and smiled at Mattie. Then he made his serious face.

"And nothing is more important than Alice," Jed said as he picked up his fork and had another bite. "Can you please pass me the salt?" James did. *Maybe Jed can take care of the family properly after all,* James thought to himself.

James considered bringing up the odd note he had found, but decided that his mother and Jed would be too concerned about his encounter with Bloody Knuckles.

"Tomorrow, James and I will start working on a house for us to have here over the winter. That will get us out of the hotel. Then, if—or I should say *when*—we go down to Yellowstone, we'll already have a claim to come back to in Bozeman." He chewed, then remarked, "Mattie, this is truly delicious."

"Thank you, Jed. Alice, James—finish your vegetables. Where do you think you're going?"

James had walked over to his satchel and reached inside.

"Here, Alice and I got this for you," James said to the preacher, jutting his hand forward with the compass. The preacher stopped eating and was overwhelmed with gratitude. Mattie looked at James and Alice suspiciously, wondering how and where they got the item, but she remained mum.

"Now we'll never lose our way," Jed said, beaming. He studied his gift.

James felt slightly uncomfortable but also proud of himself. *Maybe I should give gifts more often. This is nice,* he thought, stuffing his hands into his pants pocket. He felt the discarded, scary note from Bloody Knuckles crinkled into the creases. *Everything is going according to plan.*

"To being together! To Yellowstone!" Reverend Lawson said while raising the compass like it was a toast, then placing it delicately aside. They finished their meals with smiles on their faces and went to sleep with stomachs full of pie.

Chapter 5

THE NEWS

THE AVANT COURIER

BOZEMAN, MONTANA TERRITORY MARCH 1, 1872

YELLOWSTONE
DECLARED NATIONAL PARK!

The fall passed quickly. James and Reverend Lawson had built a house for the family, with the help of some of the boys in town. Tom and Henrietta sometimes called on them in the forenoon, bringing tall glasses of lemonade. There were long, hard days of shingling, hauling, and fixing. That took up most of James' time on the remaining warm days when he wasn't in school or at the newspaper.

Alice seemed to get a little better, or at least she didn't get worse. Every once in a while she would have a coughing spell. James became more and more eager to find out what was in Yellowstone. Certainly he wanted to help his sister, but now his interest grew further. James had his own mission: he wanted to see Yellowstone and know what business Bloody Knuckles and Red had out there.

He was glad that he'd decided not to share the note he found with anyone, but he had spent many days tossing and turning about what "the plan" might involve. As for Bloody Knuckles and Red, they'd disappeared almost immediately after arriving in town, and that was already months ago. James wondered where they went, but he was relieved that whatever suspicious deeds they were up to didn't seem to involve their town or family.

The newspaper was a good place to find out more about Yellowstone. When Alice was with Mattie, James and Tom got to read articles, look at pictures, and ask people passing through what they knew about the natural wonders. Like the Guy House, Miles' shop was a social center in the town, so they heard some fantastic stories. James found sketched maps of the Yellowstone area from recent expeditions and old prospectors. As he started to piece the geography of the region together in his head, he used one of the maps to make his own special markings. Miles said it was okay. James often stared down at his map, wide-eyed, hungry to learn about McCartney's Hotel and if there could ever be a railroad nearby like the newspapers discussed.

"Look at this. It says that water shoots into the air 40 feet high, and that there are bubbling pots of mud. What a curiosity!" Tom said. James and Tom quickly became close friends, despite their initial rocky encounter. Tom had an endless love for life's oddities, so he soon joined James in his fascination with Yellowstone. It became one of Tom's dreams to be a scientist like Ferdinand Hayden, who led a government expedition to the area. Tom always wanted to be outside. He grew rather bored sitting in a room full of tobacco smoke, and listening to gossip. But the warm days had vanished quickly and, unless he wanted a finger to fall off from frostbite, going outside for extended periods was not an option. Before James and Tom knew it, they were sitting around hot stoves wearing itchy red flannel underclothes every day, along with chest protectors and caps and buckskin mittens.

Bozeman became a giant, white blanket of frosting in the winter. There was thick snow as far as the eye could see. It would get up to ten feet deep in some places. Wind-whipped blizzards blew in from

the east and sometimes the temperature would sit at 40 below zero for a week at a time. Snowdrifts piled up and became favorite spots for kids on toboggans. James had never been so cold or seen so much snow in his life. Christmas passed, the New Year passed. And Tom continued to win the odd icicle contests, much to James' annoyance.

Before they knew it, it was the first day of March. James, Tom, and Alice walked to the schoolhouse together, as was their custom. The schoolhouse was a single room on the corner of Tracy and Olive Streets. There were only about a dozen students. Some of the students were a lot older than James, but they came because they wanted to learn to read.

On their way to school, James, Tom, and Alice would find all sorts of animal tracks: moose, elk, rabbit. Often when James and Tom turned around, Alice would be missing, having followed the tracks of an animal, or found a bird to talk to. Once James caught her reading to a lonesome chipmunk.

Alice kicked her feet in the snow, lagging behind them. "I can't wait until all the snow is gone," she said, running to catch up. She ached for it to be spring already. James mashed together a snowball.

"Think sharp!" he said and threw it at her head. She shrieked and lagged behind again, plotting her revenge.

"Nice shot," Tom said. But then his face looked long. "I tell you, I wish I could come with you to the healing waters once the weather changes."

"Well, maybe you can," James replied hopefully.

"I don't know. It's mighty dangerous out there. At least in Bozeman we've got Fort Ellis to protect us in case of an Indian raid. But out there, well, that's another story." Soldiers were stationed at Fort Ellis, three miles east of Bozeman.

"I thought the fort was established to protect people against Indian raids in the whole area. That should include Yellowstone," James said. "And besides, we'll probably be escorted by some military men."

"Anyway, Mother doesn't approve of extended holidays, and I can't leave my dad to work on the ranch alone. It's too much work and the crops are unpredictable in this weather as it is. All of the potatoes might freeze, like last year. We couldn't afford it," Tom said, trying to feel better about staying behind.

"We're not going on holiday, we're going for Alice," James said. *Well, and for me,* he thought secretly.

A snowball flew through the air and hit James square

in the shoulder with a thud. Alice laughed gleefully.

"I heard my mum tell my father that the hot springs are mostly for men soaking their private parts," Tom teased Alice. The boys started snickering.

"That's disgusting!" Alice said. She dropped her next snowball and ran next to James. "James is that true? If it is, you can bet that I'm not going."

"Tom—that's not true," James said, trying to hold back his smile. "I mean...unless they have problems with their private parts...." The boys couldn't hold back and burst out laughing. Alice chased after them, and they raced each other all the way to the edge of town.

James and Tom laughed so hard that tears came to their eyes. They reached the bridge over Bozeman Creek and doubled over, panting and out of breath. The cold air hurt James' lungs, but he had won the race.

"Let's hide and wait for Alice to catch up so we can throw snowballs at her," James said mischievously. They went underneath the wooden bridge and started gathering up their arsenal when Tom stopped him.

"Look! Indians! I think Bannock," Tom said in a loud whisper.

"How can you tell?" James asked.

"From their clothes." They wore red blankets around their shoulders and numerous other fancy trappings.

"Look, they also have red flannels, like us," James pointed out.

"But they wear their underclothes on the outside!" Tom said. They both had a good laugh. While he was laughing, the serious part of James wondered why they dressed so differently. He saw a few boys his age and wondered what their lives were like.

An old woman was being pulled with a few children on a board. Young faces peeked out of their papooses. Many stock animals huffed about.

James knew there were a few major tribes in the area—the Shoshone and Sheepeater Indians, the Blackfeet, the Crow, the Sioux, and the Bannock—but he didn't know much else. People encountered Indians fairly regularly in town, and exchanges were usually peaceable, except for the occasional horse theft. Hundreds of Indian teepees used to dot the outskirts of town, but they were around less and less. James used to think of all Indians as dangerous enemies, but now he could distinguish between hostile groups and friendly ones. A lot of the townspeople, though they never turned down a good trade, considered the friendly ones a nuisance as well.

Some people came out and started speaking to the travelers in a sign language that was common among the Indians in the area.

"Looks like they're going to buffalo," said Tom.

"What does that mean?" James asked.

"The Indians of different tribes all have an agreement with each other to come and use this area and this part of Yellowstone to hunt for buffalo. They believe that buffalo are sacred animals."

"I bet they would get along fine with Alice," James said with a laugh.

"It looks like they do," Tom said. He pointed, and sure enough, Alice was walking along as if she were part of the tribe. She stood beside a man in heavy moccasins and leggings. His hair came down in long braids. He had on a Western man's jacket. When they reached town a few of the Indians descended from their horses and looked around at the shop windows.

"Alice!" James said to himself under his breath, suddenly worried.

A group of townsmen came out with their guns, prepared for an altercation. James spotted an Indian playing with an umbrella that he had picked up from

a shop and was trying to open. It looked rather silly. Miles came out to his regular post. James felt a tension in the air.

"Alice!" James shouted to her. She saw him and smiled and came bounding toward the bridge. He grabbed her arm and pulled her down.

"Ow! What's that for?" she said, furrowing her brow.

"What are you, crazy?" James said sternly.

"No," she said. "I couldn't run fast, and I knew you'd be waiting for me with more snowballs. I figured you wouldn't be so bothersome if I was with Indians, so when I saw them coming...." Alice smiled. Tom laughed.

"What did you talk about?" James asked.

"Nothing—I don't know," Alice answered.

"C'mon, let's go inside and wait with Miles until this all passes," James said, feeling responsible. They wove through of the Indians and went toward Miles' shop. James overheard bits of conversation as he passed people on the street.

"Aren't they supposed to have a permit and an escort to pass through these parts?"

"They're supposed to be on reservations."

"Where's their military escort?"

"Tie up your horses real good, or they'll get stolen."

The church-going bell rang and the horses got jittery.

"Get off our land!" James heard someone shout from a window.

"Didn't the Indians live here before us?" James said, turning to Tom, confused.

"I reckon that we bought it from them. I think they live on reservations," Tom said.

"What's a reservation?" James asked. Tom shrugged.

"I don't rightly know. You're the one that knows stuff about people. Ask Miles."

Miles let them pass through the door under his arm as he stood in his usual position, observing the scene for a future article.

"Miles?"

"What do you want, runt?"

"What's a reservation? I mean... what happens there? Why are the Indians there?"

"They're pieces of land that the government gave to the Indians to live on so they'd get out of our way while we make nice little civilized homes." James couldn't tell if Miles was serious or sarcastic. He often wrote bad things about Indians in the newspaper, but James wondered if sometimes Miles just wrote such things because he knew it would stir folks up and they'd buy more newspapers.

"Hey James, look at this," Tom said. The week's headline was pasted on the window where James had taken the first Yellowstone article. It read: "Yellowstone Declared National Park!"

"Came in on the telegraph this morning," Miles said, writing down descriptions of the Bannock Indians and the growing crowd of townspeople. "Breaking news." Miles smacked his lips together as if the news was some kind of naughty, tasty treat to him. Alice, Tom, and James looked at each other nervously.

"Can we still go down to the hot springs if the're in a National Park?" Alice asked. James and Tom looked back at Miles in anticipation.

"Sure you can, you'll just be goin' as tourists on the property of the United States Government. So, don't plan on livin' there. Land is a funny thing these days. Well, you know that McCartney and Horr just set up a hotel out there a few months ago. I assume ya'll be stayin' with them. Not many women and children goin' out there, I reckon." He paused and thought for a moment and scratched his stubble. "In fact, I can't think of any. I only know of lonesome men goin' out there lookin' for gold. That's real wilderness out there."

Then, looking specifically at James, he added, "Make sure you watch out for that pretty face of yours." Miles chuckled, displaying his yellow-stained teeth. James rolled his eyes in annoyance.

"I guess we'll be staying at the hotel," James said, having no real idea where they would be staying. But it didn't seem like there were many options.

"You say it like you're Rockefeller stayin' at some fancy New York set-up. It's not much of a hotel. I'm not right sure they have a floor in there yet." Miles went back to writing about the Bannock for a moment but then turned back to them.

"McCartney and Horr will probably be lookin' at some trouble from the government for plantin' themselves out there now. Who knows?"

"Well, can *they* go there?" James asked, pointing to the Bannock Indians. Miles laughed.

"They're not even supposed to be *here*, boy," he answered and then whistled and shook his head. *That seems kind of unfair,* James thought.

Eventually the Indians going to buffalo passed

through the town, but it took many hours. *They'll probably make camp a few miles out and then continue on tomorrow,* James thought.

Part of James wanted to get on a horse and follow them to see where they hunted and ask them what they knew about Yellowstone and what life was like on a reservation. Instead, he and Tom and Alice just went to the upstairs window at the newspaper office and watched them ride off, with the sound of the telegraph clicking behind him.

"Alright, show's over," Miles said, manners not being his strong point. "Get out of my shop and get to school."

That night, James dreamt that he couldn't find Alice anywhere. He was running through a never-ending forest calling her name. "Alice! Alice!" Tree branches gashed his arms and legs. Then he looked down and saw that plants and flowers sprouted up everywhere his blood dropped. Drip, drip, then a stream of blood slid down his arm to the ground. The earth parted abruptly and the dirt exploded with greenery.

Soon the plants and flowers and trees were up over his head, blocking the sun. James realized that it was his blood all along that was making the forest. "Alice!" he screamed. There was nothing but an echo in dark leaves. Then James felt someone poke him on the shoulder. Alice was standing right there, behind him. She didn't speak, but buffalo horns grew right above her ears. She said in a whisper, "Help me...," and then there was a gunshot. James looked up and saw Bloody Knuckles and Red sitting in one of the trees laughing, smoke coming out of their rifles. Alice fell down dead. When he bent down to touch her, his hand passed through her body, as if she were a ghost. Then James felt a sticky red substance on his chest. He suddenly realized that the bullet had gone straight through her and pierced him right in the heart.

He woke up clasping his chest, thankful that everything in reality was safe and sound.

Chapter 6

CHIEF

The first day Mattie spotted a mountain bluebird, shiny and iridescent on top of the Chesnut Saloon, she knew it was time to start their journey down to Yellowstone. Reverend Lawson packed up his personal things and delivered his final sermon at the small church in town.

"I will be going into the infernal regions," he proclaimed. Somehow when he was at the pulpit, whether in a church or on a tree stump, the preacher gained an inner glow and confidence that James thought must have been divine, given the preacher's typically clumsy behavior. Reverend Lawson's sweat didn't form into droplets; it just rested on top of his skin like an extra layer, a holy water halo that illuminated the man underneath.

"In these nether regions, where Satan rests so close to the surface, my work will be needed even more," he said.

James was restless throughout the whole service. His back ached from sitting on the wooden bench for so long; he shuffled his feet noisily back and forth. Mattie put her hand on his shoulder to hold him still, but he couldn't help it; he was so excited to go to Yellowstone, regardless of what Jed thought of the place. He had looked at every map of the area and read every newspaper article about it. He felt like he was going to burst inside after waiting for so many months. Alice let out a little cough, and James felt a tinge of guilt for being so excited to go, suddenly remembering the real reason behind the trip. But soon he started shaking his knees again as he imagined riding on geyser streams.

About 20 people were going out to the springs with James and his family to "see the elephant." Yellowstone had many nicknames—like Wonderland—but going to see the elephant was James' favorite expression. He didn't know exactly what going to see the elephant meant, but it had something to do with going to see something strange, natural and larger-than-life. At least that's what he thought it meant. Maybe there really were elephants there. Maybe the geysers were just elephants roaming around underground spouting water out of their trunks. But that seemed near impossible. Tom would have been upset with him for suggesting something so unscientific. His feeling of excitement faded, remembering that his friend would be absent for the adventure.

The day of departure was a bit grey and cloudy. There was a fine assembly of characters in their traveling party: James, Alice, Mattie, Jed, about ten gold prospectors, an Englishman, and Dr. Aldous Kruthers of the Northern Pacific Railroad on holiday with his family.

They outfitted in Bozeman for their trip to Yellowstone. They brought lots of mosquito nets, warm clothing, coarse shoes, shotguns, rifles. Most everything was loaded into one or two wagons and the rest of the team went on horseback. Two riders came in from Fort Ellis to accompany them. They were tall, serious, and bounced up and down as their horses trotted gallantly. They brought extra supplies from the fort and went through their checklist.

"Tents," one of the soldiers said.

"Check!" the preacher announced enthusiastically.

"Blankets," said the other soldier.

"Check," came a few murmurs.

"Buffalo robes."

"Check," James said. He thought of how handy the buffalo robe had been through the winter. Alice looked away, remembering the awful gift.

"Axe," he declared.

"Check," the other soldier responded.

"I'm sad that Tom isn't here," Alice said quietly. It was as if she had read James' mind. James nodded at his sister's comment and wondered where Tom was, anyway. He was supposed to send them off on their journey and at least bid them farewell. *Maybe he is too upset and couldn't face coming,* James thought, looking around anxiously. It was almost time for them to go.

"Yoohoo!" said a woman trampling across the street, her giant behind swaying to and fro.

"Henrietta?" Mattie squinted her eyes against the sun. She couldn't make out the woman's features, but the shrill voice was confirmation enough. Casually walking behind her was Tom, pulling his horse with some extra goods.

Alice and James were so happy that they rushed

over to him. Alice threw her arms around him with joy. James thought he saw a semblance of an expression on Tom's face, but then it disappeared into his usual pallor. *What was this? Why did Tom bring his horse?* James' mind raced.

"I'm coming to soak my private parts," Tom said. Of course he said this with no expression at all, so nobody knew how to react. Mattie looked a bit worried and glanced over at Jed.

"Oh," she said, flustered. "Well, here, help with the horse...." But James knew Tom was joking. He burst out laughing.

"James, that's not polite to laugh at someone's ailment." Tom made a face and limped to pretend that he was in pain.

"Phony," James said.

"Oh, Thomas. Stop it, you," Henrietta said and gently hit him on the shoulder and rolled her eyes. He walked normal again. "Tsk, tsk," his mother said. "I tell you, Tom just couldn't stop talking about going to see the geysers. So, we had a family meeting based on your suggestion, Mattie, and we agreed that he could come down. Tom's brothers will be able to help at the homestead."

"You asked if Tom could come?" James turned to his mother, who smiled. "Thanks, Mother!" James gave her a hug.

"Will you be joining us, Henrietta?" Mattie asked.

"Heavens, no. Maybe we'll come down for a little while in August and make the trip back up together. I love you, Tommy. Be good." She gave Tom a slobbery kiss on the cheek and he grimaced. Then she swayed back toward the shops to finish her errands. It was as if she were leaving Tom for a few minutes instead of a few months.

Tom and Alice immediately started yammering about sleeping arrangements and who would get to ride the horse that was closest to the front. The supply recitation continued.

"Hatchet." Check.

"Ropes." Check.

"Hammer." Check.

"Diarrhea, check," Tom said quietly to James. James pursed his lips to stop from laughing. He looked over at his friend. He was so happy that he was coming along.

"Wheel grease."

"Check," said a small voice. It was the man who called

himself Dr. Aldous Kruthers. Aldous was a scrawny man with glasses and a bowler hat and suspenders. His two front teeth were extra large, which made him resemble a walrus. He said he worked for the Northern Pacific Railroad, but he was coming on this journey as a simple tourist from Virginia wanting to see "Wonderland." This greatly excited James. He loved everything to do with the railroads. He couldn't wait to talk to him more. James was glad that Aldous' wife came along too so that his mother wouldn't be the only lady. She was a tall, bird-like woman with a long neck and a crooked nose. Amazingly, there was something elegant about her.

"Flour." Check.

"Sugar." Check.

"Lard." Check.

They had ham, eggs in packed oats, and canned goods. The cooking supplies seemed endless: a long-tailed frying pan, a bake kettle, a coffeepot, knives, spoons, tin plates and cups.

Alice went around petting each horse on the muzzle and talking to it in preparation for the journey.

"Give my horse an extra talking to," James said. "He almost bucked me off when we were just riding around town."

She went over to James' horse and calmly spoke to it. His horse, Stomper, was tall and brown. He was a bit skittish when Alice first came toward him, but he seemed to calm down right fast with her gentle caressing. James was impressed with Alice's knack for soothing animals. The horse snorted and neighed.

"What are you doing to my horse?" James asked with curiosity.

"He is testy because he doesn't like his name," Alice said. "Who would name a horse Stomper, anyway?"

The horse starting stomping, angrily.

"Well, I can see why now—" James started.

"He's doing it because he doesn't like it," Alice said defensively. She spoke to the horse quietly again.

"He wants to be called Riser," Alice said.

"That would be terrific if he grew wings and started flying," Tom said.

"Riser is a silly name," James said. "He should be called—"

"He should be called Chief," Miles said, coming out to bid farewell. "I had a trusty horse named Chief once. The name kept both of us honest."

Alice whispered to the horse and it neighed back at her.

"That name is okay, too," she said and then was on to the next horse. James rolled his eyes but was secretly glad that he had Alice's approval.

"Chief," he said to the horse.

"I hope that name works out for you. Listen, Clifton." Miles motioned to James to lean over so he could say something in his ear. His breath smelled like tobacco and it tickled his ear.

"You be my eyes and ears out there. Write me some good letters and I'll make you my junior reporter, Yellowstone Correspondent." Miles winked, his leathery skin squeezing together for a brief moment. He patted James on the back. James loved the sound of that—"Yellowstone Correspondent!" Miles gave Chief a friendly hit on the rump and then stepped back into the crowd. "Treat him well, Chief!"

The horse neighed.

Soon enough everyone had mounted their horses and began to proceed out of town. Henrietta had finished her tasks; she came back to wave goodbye. A small group of people also stood waving and looking on. James gave Miles an especially enthusiastic wave.

"Okay, Chief. Let's go." He squeezed his heels into his brown horse and they were off. Bozeman slowly faded into the distance. He had his sister and his best friend by his side, a newly named horse, and everything he owned in a wagon. He was Yellowstone-bound and there was nothing ahead but the great wide wild.

Chapter 7

YELLOWSTONE OR BUST

The horses trudged onward. Clop, ka-clop, ka-clop, ka-clop. Neigh. Tweet tweedle tweet! Clop, ka-clop, ka-clop, ka-clop.

It was only a few days out to the hot springs, but James already felt like they were traveling to the ends of the earth. The foothills rolled out in front of the caravan in a brownish color. Elk grazed nearby. The mountains in the distance were still woven with white snow at their tips.

Some of the surrounding pine trees were as tall as 75 feet! In the thick groves, only the tops of the trees had branches. But when the party rode past some loners that had lower branches, James broke one off as he passed and tossed it next to an old animal skull. He had never seen so many animals and bones in his life.

Other than pine trees, sagebrush was the most common plant that James saw along the way. Sagebrush wasn't tall like a tree though; it was more like a stiff, dry-looking bush. It was one of Tom's favorites.

"Take this," Tom said to James when they were taking a rest from riding. He handed him a leaf from the sagebrush plant. "Break off a little bit with your fingers and smell." It had a full, deliciously fresh aroma.

This was truly Tom's playground—a land of oddities. He inspected plants and animal bones with endless fascination. He often asked the soldiers or prospectors questions when he was confused about something. He would peer out eagerly from behind his slick, black hair and absorb everything they said like a giant, pale sponge. James was amazed at how much information he could learn and then repeat back at the right time. Tom was never really good at school, but his mind was very sharp when it came to things that interested him.

They started playing all sorts of games to keep themselves occupied as the hours passed. One of Alice's favorite games was Name That Track, where they had to figure out what animal track went with which animal. The game got rather dull because they were quickly able to identify almost everything. The worst part about the game was that there was no way to really determine who was right. Sometimes when it got to a high level of disagreement they had to bring an adult over to tell them what the track was. But even then the disputes would last for hours. Tom created his own version of the game and called it Name That Poop. They had to search for scat and try to figure out what animal had left it there.

That was the one thing about animals being everywhere—there was poop everywhere, too. There was big, disc-like poop, there were little pebble poops. It was more poop than James had ever seen.

"That's a lot of scat," James commented.

"It's Poop Valley!" Alice said. They laughed together and forgot how sore their bottoms were from riding and how cold the wind got at night and how they sometimes had to eat standing up because the ground was wet from snow or rain.

Every day they woke up with the sun at four o'clock in the morning, had some parting breakfast, took down their temporary camps, and then got on the trail by six o'clock. Sometimes they stopped to go fishing.

One afternoon Tom caught 14 fish in a quarter of an hour! They cooked them and ate them, and Jed kept commenting on how it was the most delicious fish he had ever eaten. "Mighty tasty!" he said, licking his pudgy fingers.

On another day, the group spotted an old, abandoned cabin. James, Alice and Tom investigated inside and found faded newspapers from 1866 under leftover coffee grounds. The structure had probably been built, inhabited, and then abandoned by prospectors. James imagined they didn't find any gold, so with slumped heads, and pickaxes over their shoulders, they sought fortune elsewhere.

At twilight the mountains turned a majestic purple. They were no longer the silent sentinels James first encountered at Bozeman, but the royal kings and queens themselves, donning their purple evening robes.

At night, James and Tom put together their makeshift beds and wrapped themselves up in buffalo robes and blankets. They padded the ground with willow branches or whatever else they could find to make the earth more even. On clear nights, they would lie on their backs and Tom explained the constellations. They waited for shooting stars but fell asleep before they saw any. Alice sometimes read them passages from her Bible. James would doze off thinking of his father during the war and wondering if he had spent his nights lying out looking at the stars just like this, thinking about how he could make something of himself.

James knew they had made progress when they made their way down the headwaters of the Yellowstone River and arrived at the Bottler brothers' ranch. Frederick, Henry, and Phillip had set up their place near the mouth of Emigrant Gulch in 1868, and it had since become the main stopping point for people going into the park.

The ranch had many animals and good wood, water, grass, and cows. The Bottler brothers were famous hunters. They fed a lot of the prospectors and miners and whoever else found themselves passing through the remote area. They also traded skins. James and the hot springs party had a luxurious supper there with milk and butter, and they also got to sleep on a straw pile, which was rather wonderful compared to the hard ground outside.

The next night there was a storm, and Alice shuddered with every roll of thunder. She lay down close to her mother under a little shelter they had put up. James could hear her whimpering. The thunder was keeping him awake as well. He heard his mother humming softly to Alice as she stroked her hair.

"Do you know how much I love you?" Mattie said.

"As much as I love animals!" Alice said.

"More!" Mattie said. There was a loud, terrifying clap of thunder.

Alice jolted to a sitting position.

"Don't be afraid, this is all part of nature, right?"

Alice tried to nod.

"Nature is where people can go to heal their souls and their bodies. One day when you get a little older I'll read to you from books by Henry David Thoreau and a man named Ralph Waldo Emerson. They both see the beauty in nature and in the wild." Mattie went back to humming and petting Alice's head.

James never knew that his mother felt that way about nature. He had heard of those writers but he'd never thought much of them. Now he'd look them up when he got back to Bozeman in the fall. James curled up and fell asleep listening to his mother's soothing voice, and the sounds of thunder rolling away into the distance.

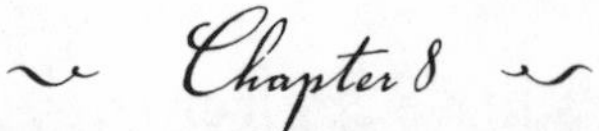

THE TERRIBLE BUFFALO INCIDENT

Clop, ka-clop, ka-clop, ka-clop. Neigh. Tweet tweedle tweet! Clop, ka-clop, ka-clop, ka-clop. James just wanted to get there! He broke off another tree branch from overhead, then he threw it into the flowing river next to him and watched the branch meander downstream. Then he smiled to himself with an idea.

"Look Alice, a snake!" He pointed to the stick. Alice loved all animals, but she had always been afraid of snakes. She tried her hardest to love them, but it took a lot of effort. James' comment caught her off guard, and she gasped in fear. Then she looked at the drifting branch again and frowned.

Realizing what it was, she said, "That's just a stick, silly. You can't fool me."

"No it's not, it's a snake. Look closer." She bent a little over her horse to look closer and then saw James holding his smile in.

"You're a no-good meanie." She trotted ahead on her horse toward the front of the line. James watched the branch dance around some rocks and he started daydreaming. Since Alice had moved ahead, he was right next to Reverend Lawson and Aldous Kruthers. The brass compass that James had given the preacher as a gift stuck out of Jed's saddlebag. He congratulated himself for finding such a useful gift at the last minute. Out of boredom, James eavesdropped on their conversation. He strained to hear snippets of their discussion over the sound of the water, which rushed beside him dancing toward its destination.

"...but the railroads have a lot of interest in Yellowstone, financially," he heard Jed say.

"I'm on holiday, Jed," Aldous said, yawning. "Do you really want to discuss the interests of Northern Pacific?"

"Well, it just seems that a town like Bozeman should be a priority for a new rail-line. Think of how many more people could enjoy this paradise!"

"Do you think I could work for the railroad one day, sir?" James chimed in.

"Why James, I didn't even know you were listening," Jed said. "What do you think, Aldous? Could this fine boy work for the railroad?"

"Let's see. . . ." He lifted his glasses. "Indeed, he looks like a fine specimen. Handsome face." James cast his eyes down in annoyance and clenched his fists out of habit.

Aldous smiled. "Why is it that you want to work for the railroad, James?"

"I guess I want to make money and be powerful and help people with my ideas."

Aldous nodded his head and frowned thoughtfully, impressed with James' candor. "That's very smart. Practical."

"He makes good marks. He's smart like his mother," Jed said. *Like his mother?* James always thought he was like his father. "And very socially-minded like her too, you better believe." Reverend Lawson turned to face him. "James, money isn't everything, you know."

"Jed, the church is able to give so much because they get so much money. Let's not pretend," Aldous argued.

"But that's not profit." The preacher was troubled by this conversation.

"Can't you make a profit and do good?" Aldous said.

"Seems immoral to me." Jed adjusted himself in his saddle. The leather creaked with the burden of his weight.

James burned red with shame. He didn't want to be immoral.

"Jed, that's just silly and backward looking. *You* must make some money preaching. The West is made of young people like James who are trying to better their lives and make something of themselves. Look at the progress we've made as moral, capable people since the war."

James hung on every word that Aldous said until they were distracted by a commotion at the front of the line.

"What's happening?" James asked to no one in particular. He rode up a little bit and saw smoke rising above the trees. The smoke was steady and dispersed, perhaps indicating a large group of people making camp.

"We're pretty close to the hotel, but we should go and investigate," one of the soldiers said nobly. "It may be Indians making camp."

James was curious. *Hostile Indians? In Yellowstone? Maybe it was the group I saw going out to buffalo,* he thought. He moved Chief around the group to the front.

The soldier continued speaking. "Someone should come with me in case there's trouble. We'll go ahead of the party to act as lookouts." The other soldier was going to stay back with the rest of the group.

"I'm coming with you," James blurted out, to the astonishment of everyone. All eyes were on him.

"James Clifton, you are going absolutely nowhere," his mother said.

"But Mother! I can ride back fast to let you know if there's anything wrong."

"Okay, boy," the soldier said. "Let's get a move on. If it's hostile Indians they've probably already had scouts out for us. Let's move." James pulled Chief out of the line, jabbed his heels in his side, and took off quickly before anyone could stop him.

"What's gotten into him?" Jed asked.

"Maybe it's the infernal regions," Aldous snickered.

James and the soldier rode up ahead of the rest of the party.

"Thanks," James said to the soldier. But the soldier wasn't thinking of James at all. He was riding toward the smoke up ahead, focused and alert.

James followed his lead. The wind was blowing his hair. The boredom of the journey was stripped away with each passing moment of the gallop. He felt like a rebel. The group was now far behind him. *This is freedom,* he thought. *This is the wild and this is nature. This is adventure!* His heart pumped with excitement.

It was all going well until they came around a bend, out of sight from the rest of the party. Chief stopped abruptly, and James went flying forward to the ground. He tumbled to the earth and scraped his elbow and knee. There were stains of grass and dirt on his clothes. Luckily that was the worst of it.

"You *are* a Stomper!" he cursed at the horse, examining his wounds. Hearing this name only made Chief more upset; he raised his white hooves into the air, came back down with a thud, then shook his mane and waved his head back and forth, neighing all the while.

"James, don't move," the soldier said. James lifted his eyes, and his frustration with Chief ceased.

There, spread out before him, were over two dozen buffalo, shot dead. Their carcasses were everywhere. The soldier pointed his gun in every direction, making sure that there was no one around. It was completely silent.

"Looks like whoever did this is long gone," the soldier declared.

James brushed himself off and stood up. He walked in between the dead animals, weaving in and out of the graveyard. The soldier dismounted and did the same. The animals were covered in different colors of brown fur. James approached one and looked it in its dead, glassy eye. The animal was even more enormous up close. James thought he could fit five of himself inside this one beast. The buffalo had friendly round ears that poked out from under its small, curved horns. It had a long, sad-looking face. The long dark brown fur under the buffalo's neck moved stiffly in the breeze, contrasting with the rest of the deadly stillness.

"Odd," James said. "Nothing was taken. The skins were even left intact."

"Looks like someone was out here hunting for sport."

"Curious that they didn't take any meat or the skins. Right?" James asked.

"Yes, strange."

"Maybe we can still make use of them," James said. "Can we take the meat or the hides?"

"It looks like they were recent kills but I'm not sure we want to risk eating bad meat. We don't want anyone laid up with nausea," the soldier said. "It may have been Indians who are coming back to get their skins.

Or maybe it's an ambush." His eyes carefully scanned the surrounding landscape; he was nervous and tense. A rider approached from the wooded, smoky area. He was waving.

"It's McCartney!" the soldier said gladly. He sat up tall and waved back and forth dramatically. The two men rode to each other and James followed.

They greeted each other. "Was this your work, Patterson?" McCartney asked the soldier.

"No, sir, we just came upon it ourselves and hoped that you could clear some of this up."

"Odd, they didn't take anything."

"We noted that as well."

"I was out hunting myself yesterday, but farther south, and I didn't hear the shots. Must have been a downright excellent marksmen to get this many." McCartney seemed unconcerned by the killings, despite being curious. There was a lot of hunting in this area, James gathered. After visiting the Bottler Ranch, he definitely had gotten that impression.

"I got a letter from Miles that you all would be arriving about today, so I hunted some mountain sheep for supper. Horr snagged a few grouse as well, so we should have a fine meal. Where's the rest?"

"They're held back a ways. We saw the smoke and thought it may have been Indians making camp."

McCartney laughed.

"That's not smoke, Patterson. You'll see what it is when you get closer. What's your name, son?"

"James Clifton, sir."

"James, why don't you come with me while our friend here retrieves the rest of your party?"

"Is there another way to the camp, sir? My sister is sensitive about animals, and I don't think it would be a good idea for her to see this."

"What a thoughtful young man you are, James. Patterson, cut around the bend earlier, at that first foothill, and you should be fine. Just follow that small stream and you'll also see some fine quaking aspen trees."

The soldier rode off, and James trotted with McCartney toward the wooded area.

"Eww. It smells like rotten eggs," said James.

"That's the sulfur from the hot springs." As they got closer James saw that it wasn't smoke, but hot steam rising from the earth.

Chapter 9

THE ARRIVAL

"This is the most fantastic oddity I have ever seen." Tom stood dumbfounded at the foot of the Mammoth Hot Springs.

"Me, too!" Alice said.

"Me, three," James agreed. They were anxious to take off and go exploring.

"Be careful there," McCartney said. "I tell you, these springs can get up to 150 degrees. I don't want any melted children on my hands."

The hot springs were not anything like James had expected. He thought there would be just plain holes of water in the ground. It wasn't like that at all. Steaming water poured over layers of earth, creating basins. It reminded James of the time he accidentally spilled a tub of bathwater down the stairs.

"How does it do that?"

"Limestone," Tom explained. "The water from the springs carries it out and leaves little bits of limestone that gather up and make those layers. They're called terraces."

"Look at all the colors. . . ." James bent over and put his face close to the surface. Little orange hair-like strands swayed in the current. James spotted almost every color of the rainbow in the different pools. Some were deep, clear, and red, while others were murky, almost like blue milk.

"I think some of the colors are from bacteria," Tom explained, trying to poke at it with a stick.

"Whoa, I think my shoe is melting," Tom said. But of course, he just stood there and watched it melt instead of moving.

"Tom, I tell you, you're crazy. Soon that will be your foot. Maybe we shouldn't walk around on this part," James said. The earth under them was fragile and crusty.

"See!" Alice said. "Take your shoes off because you're standing on holy ground." They all laughed.

"James! Alice! Tom!" James heard his mother calling. "It's getting dark! I don't want you to get too close to those springs—it's dangerous. You heard what Mr. McCartney said." She spoke with authority, but her lonesome voice sounded small in the vast wilderness. "I'm going to make a bell instead of shouting," they heard her say to Jed. James took a moment to look around and take everything in. *This is really the middle of nowhere,* he mused. He'd thought Bozeman was off the beaten path! There were probably fewer than 100 humans within 100 miles, maybe even less. Whenever he paused for a moment, he saw another critter of some sort: a jackrabbit here, a deer there.

The "hotel" was not very impressive; Miles was right about that one. They didn't even have a floor built yet. The structure was just a sod-covered log building, about 25 by 35 feet. Everyone began unloading and pitching their wall tents.

That night, they all threw a big party to celebrate their arrival. They cooked up a delicious meal and lit a large fire, and everyone told wonderful, dramatic stories. Some of the prospectors and other guests told tales about their mining adventures and encounters in the wild. James and Alice told a story about coming out to Bozeman from New York. One of the soldiers had brought a small banjo and everybody danced and sang together as the fire blazed between them. "Fan me with your fan, dear, and call me a nice young man," they sang as they clapped and stomped their feet. James never wanted it to end. They had finally arrived.

Chapter 10

HOT SPRINGS

Tom was right. It was like a holiday. Most days the group would just go hunting, pick berries, or play games. Work consisted of skinning animals and preparing meals. They were in bed soon after sundown. Sometimes, just as they did the night they arrived, they sat around a fire and told wild exaggerated stories just like Indians or fur trappers might.

James learned that some hot springs had good temperatures for bathing, mostly where the hot water joined with cool water. McCartney and Horr had gone around with thermometers and held them in the waters. They let James, Alice, and Tom try it too.

"See, that little line says it's 110 degrees Fahrenheit,"

McCartney said. "Too hot for people." They all nodded and grabbed at the thermometer, shoving each other out of the way.

"Only a year ago a group of scientists and explorers that were hired by the government passed through here to study the wonders. They showed us how to do these specific types of measurements." James looked over at Tom and saw him standing with his mouth open while he listened intently and studied the temperatures of the waters.

"Are the scientists going to come back?" Tom asked eagerly, almost drooling.

"Rumor has it that there may be an expedition at the end of the summer. If you stick around long enough you might catch 'em," McCartney said.

"Whoa!" Tom exclaimed.

"Can't you just touch the water and tell if it's hot?" Alice asked, playing with the thermometer. McCartney laughed.

"You better believe it, but this is more exact, " Tom answered. "You wouldn't want to burn your hand, anyhow."

"Maybe you could put labels up on them that tell how hot they are so people don't get mixed up and jump in the wrong ones," James suggested.

"That's a right good idea. Maybe one day we will," McCartney said.

"I hope the animals don't fall in," Alice commented.

McCartney and Horr had built small structures around some of the pools, mostly just strips of timber for sitting around and cooling off after a dip, or a strategically placed stone to sit on or put clothes on in case there wasn't a tree branch near by. The only real bathhouse was a tent located near the main basin on Hymen Terrace. McCartney built it over an oblong, human-sized hole fed by nearby spring water through a hollow trough.

Alice bathed a couple of times a day. She wasn't allowed to stay in the hot waters for too long because she was so young, so sometimes she'd just sit by the edge of a pool cross-legged. James didn't think she was getting any better, though. Her cough still sounded deep and gurgled. He grew concerned about what would happen to her if this remedy didn't work. *Maybe if she just took more time here at the springs,* he thought. *Being surrounded by all of these animals would maybe be healing enough for her,* he hoped.

When they weren't doing chores, the three of them

continued to invent new games and explore more curiosities. They found caves with fumes and smelly sulfur. There was a dead deer inside one that looked untouched. As they approached the animal in that dark, echoing cave Alice suddenly fainted. Tom and James felt lightheaded too. They decided that the caves were toxic and thereafter stayed away.

They tried to convince the adults about the deadly caves, but no one believed them. Soon they gave up and returned to more relaxing activities. They skipped stones on the springs, and even tried to cook breakfast on top of the bubbling waters! It was a rather interesting experiment, but because of the fumes, everything ended up tasting a little bit like old soggy eggs. The most amazing and revolting thing that James and Tom saw was a buffalo giving birth. A whole animal actually came out of another animal and was covered in nasty, slimy mucus. But then the baby buffalo just stood up and walked around. It was incredible. James was reminded of his dream with the miniature buffalo. He half expected the baby calf to turn and start talking to him.

One day, Tom found a mangled tree near a giant thermal mound and declared it his favorite spot in all of Yellowstone.

"You haven't even seen all of Yellowstone!" James declared.

"Well, it is my favorite spot so far," Tom answered, examining the strange curves in the tree and taking in the surroundings. James noticed that this spot was not too far from camp, but out of view of the adults. *That might be useful,* he thought.

"Let's make this place a secret hideaway," James said.

"We can tack messages for each other on the tree!" Alice said.

"Don't you touch my tree," Tom said possessively.

Eventually, they all agreed that having a secret meeting spot was a fun idea. Little did they know how handy it would be. A week or two after they had arrived, the blissful scene at Mammoth Hot Springs was clouded by some ominous visitors.

Chapter 11

PROTECT IT!

James and Tom loved trampling around the thermal ponds when Alice stayed back at the hotel with Mattie. Sometimes Aldous came along with them and they all exchanged tidbits of information. One of their favorite parts of the Mammoth Hot Springs was a 37-foot, beehive-shaped protrusion called Liberty Cap. Aldous explained that one of the government expeditions named it during the previous summer of 1871. Apparently they thought it looked like the peaked caps worn during the French Revolution.

"McCartney said there are over 50 ponds," Tom said to Aldous. "They must all be connected somehow underground. Maybe they're like an aspen tree."

"How so?" Aldous asked.

"Well," Tom explained, "when you look above ground it looks like they are all separate trees. But underneath they all have the same root system, so they're actually really only one tree."

Aldous was impressed. "Where did you learn that, Tom?" Tom just shrugged and went to look at more oddities.

James lingered for a moment and stared at the behive structure. Then he had an idea. He broke off a piece. *What a novelty!* Excitement ran through James' veins as he tromped back to Aldous to show him what he did. *Aldous will look at this and see how valuable it is,* James thought.

"Aldous, look! We can take it back to Bozeman and sell it," James said. He handed the piece to the wise traveler from Virginia. "It's like what Jed gave to me as a present. I think he called it sinter. He said it was really valuable and worth a lot."

"Hmmm...."

Aldous bit his lip with his walrus teeth and looked at the piece that James had broken off.

"Where did you retrieve this from?" Aldous asked.

James pointed to the enormous curiosity. Aldous

nodded, looking at the magnificent structure, then turned back to James.

"What do you think would happen if everybody came here and broke off a piece of this?" Aldous asked, his thumbs tucked into his vest.

James thought for a while.

"That's a trick question. There isn't anyone here. We're the only ones," James said with a smile. James felt triumphant. He saw through Aldous' scheme.

"What about when the railroad comes?" Aldous lifted his bowler hat to wipe the sweat off his forehead.

James thought again. Now he didn't know what Aldous was getting at. Was he teasing, or was he serious? Tom took the piece from James and investigated it thoroughly.

"Well, the railroad won't be here for a year or so... I don't know. Maybe other people will take my idea, and they'll try to sell their pieces for money, too. I bet they would go for a big price," James said.

"You are a young Rockefeller! That is one possibility, so let's suppose that happens. All of the young businessmen like you come out here on the railroad or by steamboat and they break off a piece and try to sell it. What then?"

James shuffled his feet back and forth. He was staring at the piece he had broken off in Tom's hands. His eyelid started to twitch.

"I know! We'll all make money, but then we'll have to come back for more or find another cone or fantastic curiosity to sell."

"Right. But what will happen to this one, this particular curiosity right here?" Aldous kept driving at something.

"It will all be taken apart?" James said with uncertainty.

"Right. It will all be taken apart," Aldous answered. "It won't be here anymore."

James looked over at the cone-shaped oddity and felt sad. He imagined this spot devoid of the entire thing altogether, missing a crown jewel of natural beauty.

"Maybe it will grow back...." he said meekly.

Tom laughed.

"What's so funny to you, Mr. Gloom Face?" James asked, annoyed.

"Nothing. Just that this took thousands of years to form." He handed the piece back to James.

Aldous picked up on Tom's cue.

"Thousands of years! My great, great, great"—he paused to think for a second then added two more greats—"great, great grandfather was alive about 300 years ago. So imagine how long ago 1,000 years was. Then imagine how long ago *thousands* were."

James felt he understood this vastness for a moment, but then the numbers escaped him. It seemed too big. There were too many greats. His brain hurt from thinking so hard. All he knew was that it was a long time ago.

"So it won't grow back for a long time," James said.

"Right."

James looked at the piece in his hand, and he suddenly felt like he had broken off a person's arm.

"It's okay. You didn't know," Aldous said, sensing James' remorse. His tone was the same as Mattie's when she consoled Alice.

"Nice work, money boy," Tom teased. He said it flatly as usual, barely even moving his mouth.

"No, no, no. James is on to something here, Tom," Aldous said. "Let's think it through. We can still make a pretty penny off of this once those railroads come. Instead of taking it apart and bringing pieces to people, we can keep it intact—meaning all together in its natural surroundings—and we can bring people here. We can have them enjoy it. But for other people to enjoy it, what do we have to do?"

"Protect it," Tom said fiercely. It was the most emotion that James had ever seen Tom show before. Tom didn't want anyone else breaking apart his new favorite oddity.

"That's right, Tom. We need to protect it," Aldous said.

"Is that why they made Yellowstone a national

park?" James asked.

Aldous smiled. He took off his glasses to wipe them off because they were getting foggy from the steam.

"That's a very nice way of looking at it," Aldous answered. "That's one of the many reasons, perhaps the most noble one. Let's go back to the hotel now, I'm hungry. I'm sure my wife is wondering where I am, anyhow."

When they walked back toward the camp, James tried to preserve his souvenir from the Liberty Cap. But detached from its source it dissolved, like sand between his hands. "Protect it," he said to himself.

Chapter 12

THE VISITORS

At the very same time that James, Tom, and Aldous were out exploring, four shadowy figures came riding toward the campsite. It was Bloody Knuckles and his son Red, accompanied by two of Bloody Knuckles' henchmen. They came upon Mattie, Alice and Aldous' wife, who sat together sewing a quilt near the hotel.

"Hello, lovely ladies." Bloody Knuckles tipped his hat, displaying his cracked knuckles. The women stood up with alarm.

"What a fine surprise to see such pristine women here to greet us after being away from civilization for so long." He leered at Mattie and then looked toward Alice. Mattie looked away and moved Alice behind her.

"Where are the gentlemen of this fine establishment? My boys and I plan to set up camp here. We've traveled a long way." Bloody Knuckles' moustache was wet with spittle. His hat was weathered. His henchmen were similarly clad in long black coats and fingerless gloves. Red stuck his chin out and just sat listening. They all had rifles slung over their shoulders, including Red. A pistol was holstered onto Bloody Knuckles' waist.

"They are out hunting and prospecting. They should be back soon," Mattie said, standing taller. Her skirts were darkened at the bottoms from trudging through dirt every day. She pulled her shawl up around her shoulders. Bloody Knuckles sensed her distance.

"We're just gonna set up camp right over there. We don't have any fancy tents like you." He scowled and went with his henchmen and Red to put out their goods and tie up their horses.

James, Tom, and Aldous had no idea

that Bloody Knuckles and Red were sitting in their camp only paces away, so when James spotted them upon his return from the Liberty Cap, he stood still, like a deer in danger. He was alarmed to find Bloody Knuckles there with his entourage and suddenly had flashes of all their previous encounters in town. *The note,* he thought. *Did they already carry out their plan?*

"Look who came back from play time," Bloody Knuckles said to Red. He pointed to James and Tom emerging through the trees that surrounded the hotel.

"What do you want?" James asked. "What are you doing here?"

"Just out to enjoy the fresh air." Bloody Knuckles smiled grossly, his lips chapped and split.

"Looks like we need to start calling him Bloody Lips instead of Bloody Knuckles," Tom said quietly to James.

"It's probably because he's a vampire," James replied.

Aldous stepped in and extended his right hand. "Nice to meet you, sir. I am Aldous Kruthers," he said.

Bloody Knuckles looked down with disgust and refused to shake Aldous' hand.

"And who are you, exactly?" Bloody Knuckles asked.

"Excuse me?" Aldous said, withdrawing his hand.

"Are you the railroad man?"

Aldous was rather surprised at the recognition.

"Why, yes. I work for the Northern Pacific Railroad. But I am not here on business right now." James found it odd to be witnessing such a formal conversation in the middle of the wilderness. A gazelle darted by innocently.

"You people are always on business, I reckon." Bloody Knuckles turned and walked away, gesturing for his henchmen to join. "We'll see you at dinner," he said with his back to them.

"My, what an odd fellow," Aldous proclaimed.

At dinner, James quickly realized that Bloody Knuckles and Red knew McCartney and Horr. They had stayed at the hotel before. The preacher also knew Bloody Knuckles and Red because they had traveled down from Helena together. But it was mighty clear from the conversation at dinner, or lack thereof, that nobody particularly liked Bloody Knuckles or Red. Nobody wanted to engage in conversation with them. James noticed that even the tough soldiers tried to evade Bloody Knuckles' gaze.

He wondered what Bloody Knuckles and Red had done to inspire such fear and dislike. James noticed that Red always carried a gun, which was peculiar for someone his age. Red didn't talk much, either, and he dressed strangely for a kid, wearing long sleeves and long pants even on the hottest days. James wondered what he was covering up. *What a creep,* James thought. He disliked Red with his whole being.

That night, Bloody Knuckles stayed up with his henchmen, drinking and shooting their guns off into the air. Alice cowered inside the tent with Mattie. Tom and James tried to sleep in the corner. They didn't want to be outside around Bloody Knuckles and his posse, whose words grew more slurred as the night progressed. They talked really loudly, and at one point they heard Bloody Knuckles shout, "Come here!" Then they heard smashing noises.

Somehow, James managed to drift off to sleep—it was amazing that he slept at all with the din of Bloody Knuckles' rowdy crew and Jed's snoring. That night he had another dream. He was lying face up, floating on a purple, boiling hot spring, his hands spread out at his sides. Then out of nowhere a giant buffalo walked over and sat on him. He saw the giant brown hairy rump come crashing down on his head, submerging him in the water. James sat up abruptly, gasping, and startled himself out of the nightmare. He took a few deep breaths of Yellowstone air to clear his mind. He did not hear Bloody Knuckles and the other men anymore. Exhausted, James let the sounds of the night insects lull him back to sleep.

The next day, Bloody Knuckles, Red, and the henchmen disappeared. That became their routine—nobody knew where they went or what they were doing during the day, but they returned almost every night, and it was always the same ruckus. The boys eyed each other nervously. Holiday time was over.

Chapter 13

THE PLEDGE

James, Tom, and Alice continued with their daily activities, but they were constantly worried that Bloody Knuckles or Red might do something extreme. Every once in a while Red's father would abandon him to fend for himself at the campsite while Bloody Knuckles and his gang went out to do whatever it was that they did during the day.

One day, when it was cold and raining outside, James and Tom took running starts and plunged into some warm bathing pools. James found it amazing that when he emerged from the steamy water his skin was so warm that he didn't even feel the cold anymore. The drizzle left little dents in the hot pool as it hit the surface. Steam rose around them, creating a haunting atmosphere.

"I'm a cannonball!" James darted and jumped into a cooler part of the spring, clutching his knees to his chest in a ball. In a lot of the places he didn't even want to stick his head under because it was so hot. Sometimes the water made James' eyes itch anyway.

"What's that, over there?" Tom swam over to James.

"I think it's a person. I'm not right sure," James said. "Hey! Show yourself!"

It was Red. He stepped out timidly from behind a pine tree. James and Tom were surprised to see him lurking around them.

"Maybe he's lonesome. Should we invite him in?" James suggested.

"Or maybe he's out to suck our blood, or drown us or...."

"I get the idea, Tom," James cut him off.

"Hey there. Why don't you come in for a swim?" Tom called out.

"What about the blood sucking?" James said in a whisper.

"It would be a mighty nasty experience," Tom whispered back.

Red just stood there and shook his head no. He was dripping wet from the cold rain, and he held his arms across his body.

"Let's get him," James whispered to Tom.

"I wonder if he has scales under those clothes," Tom said with genuine curiosity.

"Red, come on, it's nice and warm." They slowly waded their way to him. Part of James really did want Red to join them. *Maybe he will open up and tell us everything about his father,* James thought. But Red just stood there silently, staring at them with those cold, blue eyes. Tom and James looked at each other and then quickly jumped out of the water and ran after Red. He tried to get away from them but slipped on some mud.

"Come on, get into the water!" James and Tom said. They all slipped in the mud, wrestling, getting carried away by the moment.

"Get off of me!" Red shouted. *He sounds genuinely scared,* James thought. But he and Tom were having too much fun teasing and wrestling him in the mud. They managed to pull off Red's shirt, even though he was flailing in all directions. They picked him up and were about to throw him in the water when the rain washed away some of the mud on Red's body. James stopped immediately.

"Tom, stop." The mocking smiles vanished from both of their wet muddy faces. Everything was silent except the rain drizzling onto the tree branches and falling on the water.

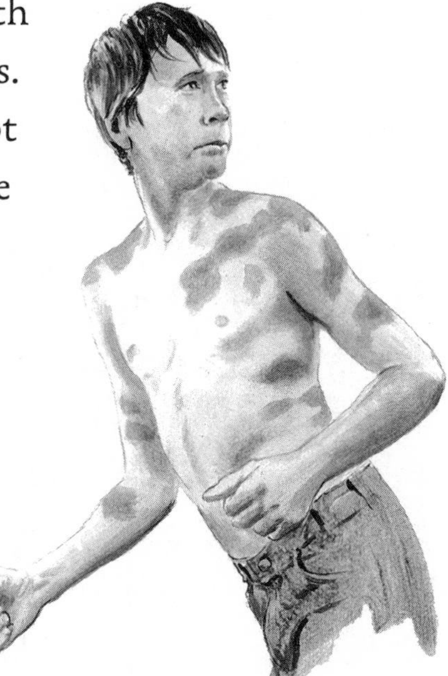

Red's body was covered in horrible bruises. He was black and blue on his sides and on his arms. Tom and James stepped away, terrified. *He really was covering up something with his long pants and sleeves,* James thought. Red quickly picked up his shirt and ran back into the woods.

"James! James!" It was Mattie, running to them with an umbrella in one hand and holding her skirt with the other.

"I heard shouting. Are you okay? What on earth is happening here?" But James and Tom were too frightened to speak.

"Wash off in the springs and then let's get back to the tent. Enough for today," Mattie instructed.

Tom and James didn't say a word to each other. Back in the tent, when they were drying, Mattie could see that something was wrong.

"Is everything okay, James?"

He could feel a lump forming in his throat. "I think I just did something wrong," he said quietly.

"Were you and Tom in a fight?"

James shook his head. He didn't want to talk about it. He didn't really understand it, or even know where Red's bruises came from, but he knew that Red was hurting, and he felt bad.

"I was just playing," James said.

"Well, I'm sure whatever it was, you will make it right. You are the most just person that I have ever known, other than your father." James put his head down in shame. He didn't feel like he was living up to those expectations.

James and Tom didn't talk about the incident at the hot springs, but it made the tension in the camp even worse. The rowdy, uncomfortable nights with Bloody

Knuckles continued. On the days when Red was left alone, he just stayed near his camping area. He never returned to the hot springs.

A week or so later, James and Alice were playing in the bushes atop a foothill when they heard the sound of something approaching below. *It might be a bear,* James thought. *Or maybe Indians.*

"Alice, you stay here. If anyone or anything comes toward you I want you to run back to camp."

"If it's an animal I can talk to it. It won't hurt us," she said, convinced of her abilities. He didn't have time to explain to her that a bear wasn't a conversational creature—just a hungry one.

James reckoned she could hear his heart pumping, but remained calm. He had to protect her. "Alice, do what I tell you. Do you understand?" He looked into her eyes. She nodded. Then she started to shake, like she was trying to hold her breath. But she couldn't keep it in. She let out a big cough. It was the kind of deep cough that gurgled like the bubbles in the hot springs.

"Who's there?" said a voice from below them.

Then James saw that it was a teenager, about 18 or so. He had bright blond hair and the side of his saddlebag had "United States Postal Service" written on the side.

"It's the mail!" James ran excitedly down the foothill toward the courier. James was excited to finally be able to send Miles some letters that he had written about his trip so far and all of their adventures. Maybe Miles would print them in the newspaper. James knew that his mother was also waiting for letters from New York and that Tom wanted a letter from his mother, Henrietta. He wondered if her handwriting was as enthusiastic as her general personality.

"Stop where you are!" The courier took out a gun and pointed it at James. James stopped in his tracks. His excitement faded. Alice let out a shriek from behind the brush.

"What are you two doing out here?" The courier asked.

"We were just playing," James answered as sternly and grown-up as he was able. "You're frightening my sister with that gun of yours. Be careful where you aim that thing."

"Apologies. It's a mighty long way to ride out alone. I don't trust anybody."

"No thieves would come all the way out here," said James. "There's nobody out here."

"Well, you're somebody. So somebody's out here."

James realized that the courier had a point.

"There's also some dangerous folks about. I've heard that. . .." The courier stopped abruptly and then looked at James with probing eyes.

"What?" James said.

"Nothing. Just rumors." The courier was suddenly awkward and fumbling. "I, um. . .just hear things and, well, I spend a lot of time alone." He examined James again but tried to avoid eye contact.

"Well, you're not far off from the hotel," James said, trying to break the uncomfortable silence. "I hope you brought some breeches for the hot pools. Alice and I can show you around."

"You're not Red, are you?" the courier finally blurted out. James was rather startled at the question. "I have an urgent letter here for either Red or a Billy Knuckles," the courier said, trying to regain his composure. "You fit the description they gave me."

James smiled. He didn't think he looked like Red at all, but he was wearing a hat. Maybe his sandy hair peeking out could have been mistaken for red in the sunlight. They *were* the same age, after all.

"Yes. I'm Red," James said, surprising even himself. He pinched Alice and she stayed quiet. "We've been waiting for that letter."

"Well, good. Now I can get it off of my hands," the courier said, fumbling again. "I don't care much for urgent mail, makes me downright nervous." He pulled out a key that was hanging around his neck, carefully unlocked the sturdy U.S. mail bag, and riffled through some letters.

"Ah. Here it is," the courier remarked, handing James the letter. James flushed in anticipation.

"Everyone will be excited to see you back at the camp," James said, trying to conceal his eagerness. "We're all waiting for letters." They walked with him a ways and then James excused himself so he could sneak a look at the letter. Alice continued to walk back to the camp with the courier.

James ran into the family tent and looked at the letter.

URGENT. TOP SECRET. It was addressed to Billy Knuckles, "or care of Red," postmarked to the McCartney Hotel in Yellowstone. It was sent from Washington, D.C., but there was no return address.

This must have been sent over a week ago knowing that Red and Bloody Knuckles would be here. I have to find out what they're up to once and for all.

James quickly tore open the envelope.

B—

How far along are you with the slaughter? I will await your answer before payment is delivered.

The slaughter? James felt the hairs on the back of his neck stand up. He remembered this word from a newspaper article he read about a group of people who had been killed. *That was it! Bloody Knuckles must be following my family. Maybe he wants to kill us! Or maybe just Alice; he seemed particularly interested in her. But why? Maybe Bloody Knuckles knew father from the war and carried an old grudge? Then again, maybe Bloody Knuckles isn't after my family at all. He did treat Aldous awfully strange. Maybe he has a bone to pick with the railroad. Or maybe... maybe he is after his own son...* James cringed to think of why Red might have those terrible bruises.

He felt a rush of adrenaline. *I cannot let this slaughter continue!* he thought to himself. *I am going to protect my family and my friends no matter what.*

Red and Bloody Knuckles were gone for the day, so avoided the mail courier, just in case someone called him James in the courier's presence and exposed his trick.

He had to speak with Tom and Alice. Alice was sitting next to Mattie, introducing her mother to the courier. Mattie was cutting up some bitterroot and prickly pear for dinner. He motioned for Alice to come. She coughed a little bit and then told Mattie she would be right back.

"What is it, Jamesie?"

He grabbed her by the hand. "Where's Tom?" James asked, looking side to side.

"Mother said that he's still looking at plants with Aldous by the springs."

"Let's go."

He darted through the camp quietly, tugging Alice by the hand.

"There they are." Tom, Aldous, and Aldous' family were strolling around and investigating plants. It was mostly Tom explaining things to everybody like a tour guide.

"This is caused by bacteria. And this here by the Opal Terrace is a. . . ." Tom saw James and Alice jumping up and down from behind a tree, motioning for him to come. Tom excused himself from the group.

"What's going on James?" Tom said plainly.

"C'mon." James led them up their secret path to the hideaway. He wanted to explain everything in a place where no one would be suspicious.

"Okay. I don't know where to start. It all began back in Bozeman. Alice, you remember when we were in the shop and Bloody Knuckles and Red were talking to you?"

"Of course. They kept asking me about the furs and about animals."

"Right." He rolled his eyes. *Everything to Alice was about the animals. There is no way that's what Bloody Knuckles and Red really talked about,* James thought.

"Well, they dropped a note on their way out and I

picked it up," James explained.

"What did it say?" Alice questioned.

"It said 'G, everything is going according to plan, BK'."

"Are you sure?" Alice said.

"Positive. For months, I kept finding and rereading the note that was in my pocket." James remembered all of those months he kept the note close to him, a mysterious secret. He felt huge relief now that he had revealed the note to Tom and Alice. He was even more eager to share everything now. He quickly handed Tom the letter that he had intercepted from the courier.

Tom read the letter aloud. "'B, How far along are you with the slaughter? I will await your answer before payment is delivered. G.'"

"How curious," Alice said.

James could tell that Tom was thinking deeply because he started tapping his finger against his leg. James explained all of his theories while Alice paced back and forth, looking down at the ground. They all stood there stewing over what these letters could possibly be about.

"Maybe we should tell mother," Alice considered.

James was overwhelmed with a feeling of

responsibility. He had to protect Alice and his mother and his best friend. *Maybe mother will make us leave Yellowstone altogether, or be mad at me for lying to the courier. What would my father do?* He questioned himself. *What did he do during the war when he knew that something bad was going to happen and only he could set it right?*

Suddenly, James had an idea.

"No, this is up to us," he declared.

He took off his shirt and ripped off a piece of cloth from the hem.

"James! What are you doing?" Alice said, watching her mother's stitching being ripped apart.

"We need a reminder. Tie this around my wrist," he said to Tom.

"This is *my* pledge. I swear that I will protect you, my friends, and my family from danger. I swear that I will do whatever I can to make things better for people through my actions. I will never make the mistake of wronging someone weaker than me ever again." He looked over at Tom, who knew James was thinking about Red.

"Are you with me?"

Alice and Tom looked at each other. "Only if you

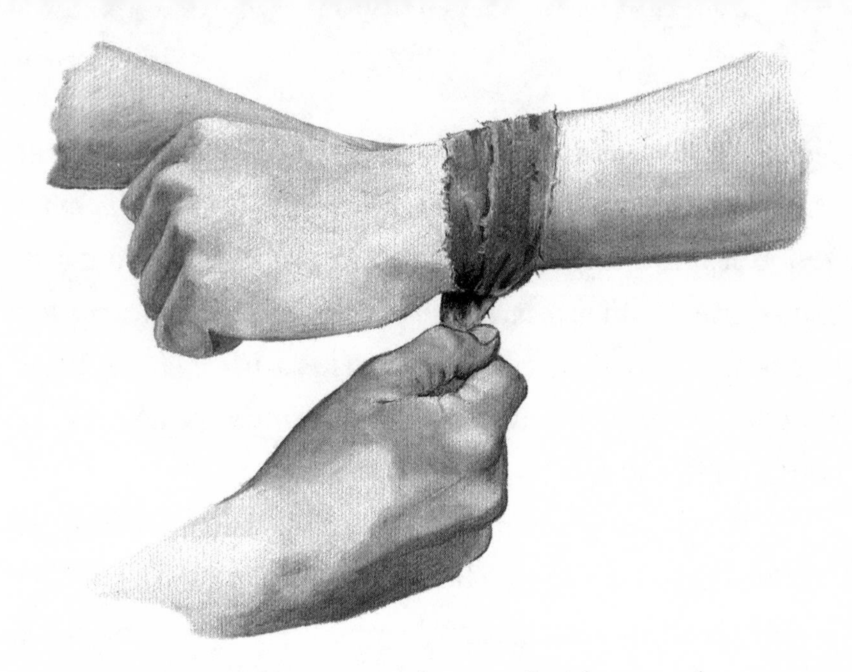

promise to protect animals, too," Alice said crossing her arms.

"Alice! This isn't about animals!" James said, frustrated.

"Yes it is. They need to be protected, too. Give me a piece." James ripped off another strip of material from his shirt, rolling his eyes. She was ruining his mission. Who could think of animals when people were going to be slaughtered?!

"Hold this," she handed her Bible to Tom, who wasn't quite sure how to handle it.

"Tie it on my wrist," she said to James. He did.

"This is *my* pledge. I swear that I will protect people *and* all of my animal family from danger. I swear to do whatever I can to make things better for animals. I will never make the mistake of killing an animal that is weaker than me, just because I can." Somehow, this made some sense to James. Instead of ruining his mission, she had actually made it stronger. Maybe it was finally how she said it. *She sounds so grown up,* James thought. He was proud of her.

"Are you with me?" James nodded and looked at Tom.

Tom handed Alice back her Bible. He took off his own shirt and ripped off a strip of material from the hem. James was surprised, once again, at Tom's concentration and passion.

"This is *my* pledge. I swear that I will protect people, animals, *and* the environment from danger. I swear to do whatever I can to try to make things better for the land's natural wonders. I will never make the mistake of senselessly destroying the earth or abusing it, just because I can." He looked at James. James thought of the sinter and realized exactly what Tom meant. *Protect it,* he reminded himself. The mission was strengthened even more by Tom's pledge.

"Are you with me?" Alice and James nodded. They all looked down at their wristbands. *We're like the aspen tree with many branches, but one root system,* James thought.

"This is our pledge," they said together. James felt that this moment was the beginning of something important, something meaningful. He knew this pledge meant they were seeking something beyond themselves, a higher code of conduct that would impact their lives and maybe even the lives of others. He was no longer that lonesome tumbleweed drifting out alone. His best friend and his sister were there with him, and he even felt like all the trees around him and all the animals were there with him too. He felt connected to something greater.

"Okay, then. Let's figure out how to deal with Bloody Knuckles," James said. They sat down and plotted beneath the canopy of trees, with the birds and groundhogs as their only witnesses. Then they heard the bell for dinner.

Chapter 14

DEATH

James crossed his fingers, hoping that the courier would leave before the sordid father-son pair returned. As it was, James found himself avoiding the blonde deliveryman—around meals, around hunting. He feared that someone would call him by his real name in the courier's presence. Each time James was spotted by another camp inhabitant, he tried to speak first to avoid revealing his true name.

James, Alice, and Tom loaded up on defense supplies. They had slingshots, ropes, and rock piles. They needed to prepare for the worst. Next, they would uncover as much information about "the plan" and "the slaughter" as possible.

They began by re-examining all of the information they had to date on Bloody Knuckles. Miles, back in Bozeman, had told them a few things, but nothing seemed particularly helpful. Perhaps the place to start was by asking the others in camp what they knew—obviously they were uncomfortable around Bloody Knuckles for a reason.

The preacher was their first subject. They asked him what he knew about Bloody Knuckles and Red from his journey down from Helena.

He sat eating some jackrabbit meat while talking. "Strange pair. Mostly just kept to themselves. Sometimes they would be rowdy and there would be some altercations, but generally we tried to avoid them." He took another bite from the meat around the bone.

They asked the two soldiers from Fort Ellis as well.

"I heard that they've escaped hangings in a few towns now, you'd better believe. They're probably out here because they think no one can get them. But we wrote letters to the rest of the boys back at the Fort and all of Bozeman knows he's out here. Everyone is just waiting for him to make one bad move so we can arrest him once and for all."

"What did they do?" James asked, as Patterson and the officer inspected their horses' hooves.

"I don't think it's just one thing. Some say he is working for someone else, that he's hired and paid a good amount to do someone else's dirty work—a mercenary."

"Has he ever harmed anyone?"

"I can't say for sure. He's definitely robbed a few trains. Hard to say why he needs to rob anything if he's getting paid so much. One thing is for sure—he's a sharpshooter. Never misses, I'm told. Quite the hunter as well. I don't care much for him, despite his abilities. Why are you snoopin' about him anyway, James?"

"No reason. Just curious is all," he said smiling casually. James felt like a reporter asking all of these important questions, keeping his motives to himself. He couldn't wait to write to Miles about the experience.

Unfortunately, most of the questioning led to dead ends or just more of what they already knew. Nothing seemed relevant to the notes or to their particular camp, and some of the information just confused them.

"Slim pickins'," Tom said. He had a new scab on his elbow that he started poking at. They all looked at each other and shrugged.

It came down to simply waiting for Bloody Knuckles and his men to return and make a move.

Finally that night, after what seemed like an eternity, Bloody Knuckles, Red, and the henchmen returned. To make matters worse, it started hailing, so the courier decided to stay another night. *Uh oh,* James thought. It was twilight as the grubby crew made their way toward camp. James, Alice, and Tom decided that the best thing to do was to keep Red occupied and away from the courier.

"Get him out of camp. You can find out more from him, keep him away from Bloody Knuckles in case he's in danger, and avoid an uncomfortable encounter with the courier," Tom said.

"Okay," James agreed. James was also secretly hoping that he could use this moment alone with Red to apologize for trying to force him into the springs on that rainy afternoon.

James walked nervously over to where Bloody Knuckles and his gang had set up camp. There was a stench of old liquor and meat that made James' stomach turn. Between the smells and his nerves, James thought he might be sick.

"What do you want?" Bloody Knuckles said.

"I...I was wondering if Red maybe wanted to go hunt some grouse with me. See, I don't have a gun, and I hear he's a good shot."

Red stood silently, watching the exchange.

"Red only hunts with me." Bloody Knuckles snarled defensively. One of his henchmen looked up from sharpening his knife on a leather strap and took a puff of tobacco. Bloody Knuckles looked down at Red and whispered something in his ear. Red nodded.

"Fine. Only if Red wants to go. We've had a mighty long day already, and I expect we'll all be eating soon. Kind of a strange time to want to hunt."

"The animals come out more when the sun starts to go down," James said, surprised at his ability to confidently improvise.

"You want to go?" Bloody Knuckles looked over at Red with a fiery intensity. "Remember what I told you about knowing who your friends are."

Red nodded, never looking his father in the eyes. Bloody Knuckles pushed him forward.

"Get out of my sight."

As they walked away James saw the blond courier approaching Bloody Knuckles' campsite. Tom was next to him trying to make conversation. *Good effort, Tom,* James thought, as Tom walked backward and physically tried to divert the courier away from Bloody Knuckles. But James could see that the courier was just annoyed and walking around Tom. He wasn't responding at all, and he looked determined.

"Let's get our horses," James said, returning his attention to Red.

"My father said that I can't go too far, so I can't take a horse. We can hunt just as good without them anyway, I reckon. We just have to be quiet."

James smiled with his lips closed. It was the first time he had ever heard Red speak, other than his screams at the hot springs.

As they rushed off over a foothill and behind some trees, James looked back to see the courier and Bloody Knuckles talking. Tom abandoned his efforts and slunk back, feigning interest in some insects. The courier appeared to fumble again in Bloody Knuckles' presence, then he turned and pointed in James' general direction. James and Red hurried off into the woods.

Before they knew it, James and Red could no longer hear the voices in camp. The sounds of the henchman's knife being sharpened against the leather strap faded away and now it was only chirping magpies.

"Say, Red, I'm really sorry about what happened at the springs the other day. Are you okay?"

"I don't know what you're talking about," Red said, quickly moving ahead.

"But..." James began.

Look!" Red pointed. Just over on a grassy foothill there were four stray buffalo. "Watch this," he said. "Follow me."

They crept over the side of the foothill, laying low to the ground. Red took his rifle off his back. The earth smelled strong and grassy under James' nose. He was frustrated. How could he reconcile, let alone apologize, if Red was ignoring the fact that the incident by the springs had even happened? They circled around through the trees, finally stopping at a place Red considered a good spot. He crouched down and squinted one eye and focused intently on one of the monstrous creatures. It was difficult for even grown men to hunt buffalo, but Red was doing it with ease. Suddenly there was a clang and a shot fired in the air. He hit the buffalo in the chest then prepared for another shot. CLANG! He hit the buffalo in the head. It fell down groaning.

"Wow!" James said. "You got him!" All thoughts of discussion faded away. James was caught up in the excitement of he hunt, his blood pumping violently through his veins.

Red smiled a toothy grin. The giant carcass was lying on its side, defeated. But Red wasn't finished. He was actually aiming for a second buffalo and he shot it in the rear as it ran away. He fired again, and the second buffalo went down. Now there were two massive buffalo lying on the ground groaning in pain. James suddenly felt his excitement turn to anxiety when he realized how dangerous and bloodthirsty Red could be.

"Okay, I think that's enough," James said, shocked at Red's shooting skills and fearlessness. "We should finish those two off to stop their suffering and then get the skins and the meat." He looked down at his wristband.

"No, let's get the other two!"

Red darted ahead. James looked back at the dead buffalo. He thought of Alice's pledge and his promise.

Then it suddenly dawned on him.

"Wait!" he shouted as Red bounded up the mountainside.

"*You* killed those dozens of buffalo north of the hotel, didn't you?" James blurted out. Red stopped. There was no sound but the breeze. James felt like the whole earth stood still.

"I don't know what you're talking about," Red said. They stood ten paces apart. It was like a cowboy showdown.

"You killed all those buffalo for no reason, didn't

you?" It all pieced together in his head like the maps he looked at in the newspaper office. "I'm such a fool! This whole time I thought the slaughter was about people, but you're out here to slaughter the buffalo!" James shouted. He heard the sound of approaching hooves beating the ground, and he turned around. Bloody Knuckles was atop a horse, riding violently toward them. James realized it wasn't just any horse — Bloody Knuckles was riding Chief! There was nowhere for James to run.

"Very smart little bugger we have here, huh, Red? Looks like he needs a good beating," Bloody Knuckles spat as he trotted up, circling around James, who eyed Chief cautiously. James tried to communicate with his horse, like Alice had.

"You know, it's not nice to steal," James said to Bloody Knuckles, who was pressing hard on his horse.

"I believe you have something of mine, as well. You know, it's illegal to open someone else's mail." He glared at James from atop Chief like a demonic knight. James felt like it was Bloody Knuckles who possessed all the infernal descriptions of Yellowstone.

James took the urgent letter from out of his breast pocket. He looked to the mountains for support, but the giants stood there quietly. He looked back toward where Bloody Knuckles came from, but there was no hint of other travelers. James' ears remained perked, but there were no sounds other than his own beating heart and the horse's panting nostrils.

"Here, sir," he said, his hand shaking.

"Bring it to me." James looked over at Red again, who just stood there. James walked to the horse tentatively.

"Hand it to me!" Bloody Knuckles declared. James lifted his trembling hand as Bloody Knuckles snatched the letter away from him. Then he lifted the back of his right hand and smacked James across the face. James tumbled to the ground as he tasted the metallic blood in his mouth. His mind went dark for a moment, but then he returned back to consciousness. As he opened his eyes, James saw the dirt of the ground and the crushed grass. He saw the dead buffalo lying up ahead. He rolled onto his side and screamed to Bloody Knuckles.

"I don't understand why! Do you have some sort of sick competition going to see who can kill the most buffalo for sport?"

"No, but that sounds like fun. And we wouldn't be the first to do it."

James thought of hunters who shot at the buffalo from the trains just for fun.

"If not that, then what?"

"Well, well, well. We have our junior reporter, a miniature Miles. Have you seen any Indians around here?"

"Not many," James said, confused. "They're mostly on reservations."

"But they come out sometimes and interfere with us. Why? Because they are hunting buffalo. So how do you get rid of the Indians? Get rid of their food source—their silly sacred animals."

Alice was right! It was the animals all along.

"But who told you to do that?"

"I guess some things will just have to remain a mystery, won't they? That wake-up slap was just for fun." Bloody Knuckles lifted his gun.

"You can't shoot me," James said, dumbfounded.

"Why not? A simple hunting accident." Bloody Knuckles lifted his gun to shoot when suddenly a rock went flying in the air and hit the horse. The horse bucked and Bloody Knuckles' shot skimmed past James' head. It was Red! Red had saved him!

"You worthless scat! I'll deal with you later!" James used the moment to run, or, to put it more accurately, he tumbled and rolled down the side of the hill, with brief flashes of Bloody Knuckles sitting on Chief, in pursuit. James landed in a muddy pit at the bottom of the hill in the middle of an aspen forest. The thin trees were tightly packed together. James jumped to his feet and wove in and out of the trees, jumping over logs, zig-zagging and making it difficult for Chief to get through. He ran as fast as he could until he was out of the forest. Bloody Knuckles was close behind him.

As he emerged from the forest, the earth underneath him started to change consistency. Suddenly, James' leg burst through the crusty ground to a shallow hot spring and his leg was scalded by the splash.

"Ahh!" he screamed. But he was forced to recover when he looked up and Bloody Knuckles was approaching. In a miraculous flash, James had an idea. He tried to narrow his body and hide behind the aspen tree. Bloody Knuckles clopped forward, faster, faster, faster, he was getting closer. *Just a few more feet,* James thought anxiously. *Just a few more feet.* Finally, when Bloody Knuckles was close enough for James to look him in the eye, James screamed to his horse.

"Hey, Stomper!" The horse immediately got agitated and galloped past James at top speed, then stopped very abruptly. Bloody Knuckles went flying over the top of Chief into the center of a boiling hot spring.

"AHHHH!" Bloody Knuckles shrieked as he fell into the infernal cauldron.

James ran after him to see what happened. He had hoped that Chief would toss Bloody Knuckles off the horse, but he didn't realize that Bloody Knuckles might land in a hot spring.

I can't just leave him to suffer in there, James thought. *He might die.* He heard Bloody Knuckles splashing. *I vowed to protect people, just like my father had protected people. I know exactly what my father would do.* James turned around and tried to find a way to help the flailing Bloody Knuckles.

"Swim this way!" James tried to find something to help him but couldn't. He couldn't get any closer, or he would fall in himself. His leg was still stinging from where it had contacted the boiling water.

Bloody Knuckles didn't hear him. He just continued thrashing and then his screams started dying down. Slowly, he grew still. James knew he couldn't help. He called his name, his real name. "Billy! Billy!" But Bloody Knuckles had disappeared under the water.

James stood stunned for awhile; he didn't know for how long. He finally whistled for Chief and rode away from the gruesome scene as fast as he could.

As he rode with the wind in his face, he couldn't contain his tears. *Maybe it's just the wind making my eyes water,* James thought. He rode back up to where Red had been, but he was gone.

His thoughts raced. *Could I have done something else to save Bloody Knuckles?* He couldn't shake the image of Bloody Knuckles thrashing and his boiling skin. James just wanted to get back to camp and fall into his mother's arms and tell her what happened. *Was it my fault? Did I kill Bloody Knuckles?* James spun all of his thoughts in a web around his head. *No! I tried to save Bloody Knuckles, even after he tried to kill me.*

He was traumatized by what he saw. James trembled. He suddenly had a moment of being enormously thankful for his life. He had come close to being shot like those buffalo groaning on the ground.

He had to write to Miles. He would tell him everything. The whole town would find out. How could he explain to everyone at camp what happened? There was so much to tell Mattie and Jed and the Krutherses, and the soldiers!

To James' surprise, as he rode up to camp the two soldiers were riding out toward him.

"Come with us right away," they said.

They all dismounted from their horses. James didn't realize that he must have looked a wreck. Mattie came running over to him and hugged him. Jed looked choked up as well. Tom stood behind them with his head hung down. The courier was there as well.

"Tom told us everything, James." Mattie wept and held on to James as tightly as she could. Then she looked up at the soldiers, but they shook their heads and frowned. *Why would they do that?* James wondered. Mattie started crying more, so Tom started to speak instead.

"Red came running back into camp. Before we knew what was happening, the henchmen packed up their goods and rode away. I knew something bad had happened. I couldn't find your horse anywhere," Tom said, looking even paler than usual. "And then I went to find Alice. . . ."

"But there's more," James cut him off. "I have to tell you what happened, Mother." James was so happy to be back in his mother's arms. But Mattie just sobbed uncontrollably, tears flowing all over James' torn shirt.

James tried to gather himself for her sake.

"I'm okay. Look, I'm okay."

But Mattie just clutched him tighter and sobbed more. Then she pulled back, looked at him, shook her head and said, "It's Alice."

Chapter 15

ALICE IN WONDERLAND

They looked everywhere for Red, but he had vanished along with the henchmen, and, strangely, a few of the prospectors as well.

Jed insisted that they go back to retrieve Bloody Knuckles' body and give him a proper burial. So James led the preacher and the Fort Ellis soldiers to the exact spring. Jed insisted that James go back to the camp while they searched for the body. They eventually found it and carefully managed to fish him out without injuring themselves. They created a small grave nearby and marked it with a stone. By the time the sun set, the men had toiled for many hours. They came back into camp with hungry stomachs and clouded minds.

The following day Jed conducted a funeral. He sang some hymns and prayed for the tainted soul of Billy Knuckles. "He was a man who was lost in life. Hopefully, in death, his goodness will be found." Everyone lowered their heads in a moment of respect for life, even in the midst of such evil.

James couldn't sleep well at night because he kept hearing Bloody Knuckles' dying shrieks in his mind. He knew he would be haunted by them for a long time.

But the main reason he couldn't sleep well was because of Alice. When his mother had finally calmed down enough, she explained that Alice had disappeared. It was Tom who first went looking to find her, and he came upon her Bible spread open on the ground. He called and called, but she was nowhere to be found.

"We thought that she may have been with you, but when you came back alone, we knew for sure that she was missing," Tom explained.

That's why the soldiers shook their heads, James thought.

Everyone left at the hotel spent the next few weeks searching for her nonstop, but there was no trace of her. Mattie was inconsolable. She walked around camp like she was the one that was missing. She would just wander around, searching. Jed did his best to keep her spirits up.

One stormy afternoon, another mail courier arrived with letters. The family received a large bundle of condolences from family and friends back East and from Bozeman. James received a letter from Miles along with a copy of the most recent newspaper. He sat in the tent and read it.

Dear James,

I hope this finds you feeling in better spirits. We all know that you did some mighty brave things out there in your dealings with Billy Knuckles. Don't regret your actions for one minute, I tell you. He was a terrible man and he deserved a terrible death. You better believe you did more than most grown saints would have done to try and save his sorry soul — more than I would have done, I reckon. Most people are celebrating you as a local hero for what you've done.

The last thing that James felt like was a hero. He didn't want people to adore him for killing somebody. He wanted to be a hero for exposing Bloody Knuckles' wrongs. He appreciated what Miles was trying to say, but he cringed and read on.

All of Bozeman is awful distraught over the disappearance of your sister. The weather here has been fine, a little stormy. It's starting to get into the long days of summer. The ladies are all walking around town with their parasols. The McDonald boys have been coming over to help out here and run errands since you've been gone. The town is busting out more and more every day now. There are wagons of people that keep passing through and new homesteaders are coming out to see what they can do with themselves. The paper is surviving, hasn't gone extinct yet (although Darwin would say it's definitely in danger). As you know, we have to write to what people might buy. Unfortunately, most people aren't too upset about buffalo killing. It's kind of the habit for us out here so I couldn't run a whole piece on it like you wanted me to. You'll just have to keep on convincing people that it's a worthy cause. I'm sure you'll do just fine at that.

I'm sorry that I couldn't put too much in about your sister — Dr. Wright told me that too much negative press about Yellowstone would disrupt tourism. So, we're trying to keep it out of the spotlight until we know more about what happened.

They started a little library association here, some of the boys did, and I'm sure you'll be happy to read up on all those topics you asked me about. There is plenty on Thoreau and Emerson and all those other Eastern romantic-like folks. (Ask me about Southern writers one day. Those guys will really knock your socks off!) I hear that your family will probably be coming back up to these parts soon if there is no more sign of your sister. We'd be happy to have you. Say hi to Tom and all.

Your loyal friend,

Miles

James opened the paper and read some of the headlines. "Ulysses S. Grant" re-elected. There was a spread on the death of Billy "Bloody" Knuckles. James mumbled aloud to himself: "Born in Missouri, Billy Knuckles swayed between an honest living and a life of lawlessness. His first crimes were robbing stagecoaches, and later he took to robbing trains. Knuckles married Mary Fontaine in 1858 and had a son named Reggie, commonly known as 'Red', in 1861... Knuckles soon left his young wife and son and turned temporarily to an honest living as a saloon keeper in Illinois. In recent years, he supposedly abandoned a life of crime, once again, to be a buffalo hunter. He was quite accomplished, killing approximately 1,000 buffalo in just a few years." James skimmed over the gruesome and embellished details of Bloody Knuckles' death and continued reading at the bottom of the article. "His gang of accomplices, commonly known as the Long Coat Gang for their often-worn long black coats, is also known for their violent lawlessness. The Long Coat Gang includes Charlie Slinger of Dakota and Steel-Fist Farley of Texas. Their current whereabouts are unknown." James sighed, taking in a deep breath.

There was also a tiny blurb in the middle of the newspaper about Alice going missing.

GIRL MISSING!

A young girl from the Bozeman area followed animal tracks out into the wilderness and has gone missing. Already ill, there is little chance that she will survive in the wild on her own. Ladies, please watch your children carefully and remind them that although animals look nice and fluffy, they can be quite dangerous.

There was nothing about the possibility that she could have been abducted—either by the prospectors or Bloody Knuckles' henchmen. *Maybe she was even with Red or Indians. They didn't find any remains, so it seemed unlikely that it was an animal attack. But it was still a possibility.*

"James, why don't you get outside for a little while? It looks like the rain is clearing up. I have a trusty compass here in case you lose your way," the preacher offered.

James knew that Jed was trying to be nice and helpful, but getting lost reminded him of Alice. Jed realized this and tried to cover it up, but fumbled with his words.

"But of course you wouldn't get lost. . .well. . .you know. But it was such a nice present you gave to me. . . and. . .."

"Thanks, Reverend. I'll hold onto it just in case." James put the compass in his satchel, then tried to give a little smile as he tossed the paper next to his sleeping mat and walked out.

James sighed as he trudged through the woods toward the hideaway. One of the worst things about the whole situation was that James never got to tell Alice that she had been right. Tom had been right too. He couldn't just protect humans alone. Everything was interconnected. The bad things being done to the Indians were also being done to the animals. The bad things being done to animals were because people were fighting over land. The railroads that he loved so much could bring people out to see nature's wonders, but they also destroyed Indian lands. The people, the animals, and the land were all like that aspen tree—many parts seemingly separate on the surface, yet actually connected by the same root system.

What would happen if there were no more buffalo? James wondered. Jed said that "the West wouldn't be settled for 500 years" and that "there were more buffalo than people in America." *But what if it did happen? What if we killed every single buffalo?* James couldn't shake the image of the suffering animals just lying there. *And for what?* He had to tell Alice. He had to tell her that he understood why she cared about the animals so much and why she was right.

The skies were clearing up overhead. James arrived at the hideaway, where a mountain sheep stood grazing. They eyed each other for a moment and then the sheep scampered off.

James sat down. He furrowed his brow and thought of all the work ahead that he and Tom had to do. Amidst all of this tragedy, he was still thankful for so many things. Not only was he thankful for his life, but he was also thankful that he had found his friends and knew his cause. Amidst all the chaos and death, nature and animals and people were thriving with life and possibility. He twirled his wristband around. But how could he do any of it without Alice?

"Father, if you can hear me, I didn't forget my promise to you. I hope that I am living up to your expectations. Even though I failed in protecting Alice, I haven't given up. Mother said that you were always patient in your work. Maybe in time everything will come together. Some things already have."

He heard the sound of branches cracking. *Maybe it was Alice.* James stood up, imagining her little bangs. *I was just talking with some coyotes who took me back to their den,* she would say.

"Hey." It was only Tom. James sat back down again.

"This is madness," James said. "I can't believe we're going back to Bozeman. We have to keep looking for her."

"James?" Tom looked at him. James looked up from playing with the strings of his wristband. "You did really good." James just looked back down and picked up a branch from between his feet.

"I think Alice is still alive," Tom said.

"She was getting sicker, Tom. She maybe wouldn't have lived even if she was still here." That was the first time that James even admitted that thought to himself. It made him start to choke up just thinking it.

"Well, I'm not going anywhere. I think we haven't looked hard enough. And, we can't carry out our pledges without our third group member." James smiled a little as Tom thrust his hand forward and showed his scraggly shirt strip still tied around his wrist. He never had to explain things to Tom.

"And you can't go back to Bozeman before that eye heals, anyway. It would give Miles too much satisfaction to see your handsome face all black and blue," Tom added wryly. James laughed a little and was reminded of the throbbing pain that still lingered from where Bloody Knuckles had hit him.

"Let's go jump in the hot springs before dinner," Tom said.

"Okay," James said.

"I'll race you there."

"You'll lose."

"That's what you said about finding the most curious icicle. And what happened there? You lost. All winter long."

They were quickly up on their feet and running. James plunged into the water then slowly drifted up and floated on his back. He stared at the open blue sky with its wispy, whimsical clouds, and he started plotting how they would find Alice. They would have to go deeper into Yellowstone.

Back at camp that night, he and Tom prepared for bed.

"Tom, about what you said before, about Alice...." he tried to keep his voice down so that Mattie and Jed wouldn't hear. "I think we should look for her. We know her better than anyone, and we know where she'd likely go or what she'd likely do."

"I agree," Tom answered, fluffing up his bed and creating a small headrest for himself.

It was a cool, dry night. James had been so afraid of going to sleep at night, but now he was comfortable with the wild. They had gotten used to the coyotes and bears lurking around the campsite. He wondered how he would ever go back to sleeping in the quiet, still, stuffy rooms of a town.

"We should probably look for her as soon as we can. Every moment gone is another that she could be in danger," James whispered.

"What about them?" Tom jerked his head toward Mattie and Jed, who were also speaking quietly to each other in the corner.

"I don't know," James said.

"We can't run away just the two of us; we'd need more supplies and a guide," Tom said.

"I have all of those Yellowstone maps memorized. And with your science skills. . . ." James started.

"We should at least get one of the soldiers to come with us," Tom said.

"Maybe," James answered and laid down with his hands folded behind his head. He could see some stars through the open tent trap. He was reminded of a verse that Alice would sometimes read at night when she looked at the stars: " 'Lift up your eyes on high, and behold who hath created these things.' "

He saw a shooting star as he drifted off to sleep. He fell into a deep, heavy slumber and was awoken by a voice whispering in his ear: "James, get your things. Let's go."

to be continued...

The Real History

Virginia Cascades, Yellowstone National Park. (1905)

left: Fishermen in Yellowstone. (circa 1880)

below: Members of the Bannock Tribe in the Idaho Territory. (1871)

above: Guard house on officer's row in Yellowstone. (1917)

right: Early tourists gathered around Yellowstone's 'Giant Geyser'. (circa 1880)

A Defining Event

Yellowstone National Park became the world's first national park on March 1, 1872, marking the first time in recorded history that a country set aside land and wildlife to be forever preserved and protected.

Supported mainly by railroad companies like the Northern Pacific (Aldous Kruthers' company) and with assistance from private and government-led expeditions conducted by scientists, President Ulysses S. Grant signed a law declaring that approximately two million acres of land be set aside "for the benefit and enjoyment of the people."

Yellowstone's founding triggered a worldwide national park movement and greater interest in land preservation and wildlife protection. Today, thousands of national parks and preserves have been established in over 100 countries. But it took many years of learning how to properly manage natural wonders and revolutionary ideas about wilderness in order to get to this point.

Yellowstone's Explorers

Expeditions set out to explore and document Yellowstone's vast and mysterious landscape, beginning in 1869. These expeditions helped to influence the public and politicians to establish Yellowstone as a national park. In 1872, an expedition documented the presence of women and children around Mammoth Hot Springs "taking the waters," which was a practice that people engaged in at the time to try to cure various illnesses.

Newspapers

In the 19th century, newspapers were the main way of receiving information about the world. The first newspaper in America appeared in Boston in 1690. By the end of the Revolutionary War in 1783 there were forty-three newspapers in print. After the Industrial Revolution, newspapers continued to experience significant growth—being that they were easy to produce and cheap to buy. By 1850, there were 2,526 titles and by 1880 the census recorded 11,314 different papers! During the Civil War people craved fast information. Often, the newspapers weren't as factual as we imagine, because their owners directly influenced what the newspapers wrote about.

Monthly publications, such as *Harper's, Atlantic Monthly,* and *Scribner's* all competed for frontier tales and reporting. In 1871, *Scribner's* ran the story "The Wonders of Yellowstone" with illustrations by Thomas Moran and tales from Nathaniel P. Langford. This article, among others, was pivotal in creating awareness and enthusiasm about Yellowstone.

The Bozeman Avant Courier

The first Bozeman newspaper was titled the *Montana Pick and Plow*, established by Horatio N. Maguire in the winter of 1869-1870, which later became the *Avant Courier*, owned and published by Dr. Wright. The paper often ran accounts about visits to Yellowstone, and enthusiastically heralded the coming of the Northern Pacific Railroad as well as Yellowstone's natural wonders. While "Yellowstone Declared a National Park!" on pages 51 and 63 was not a real headline, national papers such as *The New York Times* did note the congressional passage of the bill creating Yellowstone as a national park.

Jay Cooke

The founder and visionary of the Northern Pacific Railroad, Cooke was an instrumental figure in establishing Yellowstone as a national park. He largely funded the original Hayden expedition of 1871 to Yellowstone, supplementing Congress. He felt Yellowstone would provide the railroads with a profitable tourist destination, as much as the railroads could benefit the Park. Unfortunately for Bozeman, Jay Cooke went bankrupt in 1873, which prevented the completion of the railroad into the Gallatin Valley until the 1880s.

> By means of the Northern Pacific Railroad, which doubtless will be completed in the next three years, the traveler will be able to make the trip to Montana from the Atlantic seaboard in three days, and thousands of tourists will be attracted to both Montana and Wyoming in order to behold with their own eyes the wonders here described. —*Nathanial Langford, Scribner's Monthly, 1871*

A Troubled Beginning

It may be hard to believe now, but in the 1870s, most people thought the "West" and "the frontier" would take hundreds of years to settle. Diaries from the 1870s describe women using axes to hack pieces of sinter as Yellowstone souvenirs, as the fictional character James initially tried to do. Nearly everyone who entered the Park in 1872 shot animals and birds as they pleased. Visitors to the Park in the early and mid-1870s wrote in their journals that killed animals could be seen everywhere. People thought the wilderness was unending — the way people think of outer space today — and that wildlife was so plentiful that it could never become extinct. Such misperceptions led to tragic consequences, especially for American bison and the Native American population.

Hunters Bad Mat, Long Ole, Sleepy Hank, and Scowling Charley display their haul of over 100 birds. (1880)

Yellowstone's Landscape

Yellowstone has a vast and unique landscape. It is larger than the states of Rhode Island and Delaware combined. The Park contains over 10,000 hot springs, which is half of the hot springs in the entire world. This includes the largest concentration of geysers on Earth! The most well-known geyser is "Old Faithful," which shoots thousands of gallons of extremely hot water over 100 feet into the air about every hour and a half.

right and below: Old Faithful Geyser

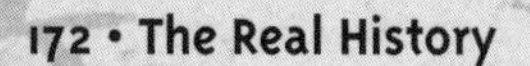

Huge volcanic eruptions occurred in Yellowstone around 2 million, 1.3 million, and 640,000 years ago. The underground magma heat that powered those eruptions still powers the Park's hot springs today. Nearly every day, there is an earthquake in Yellowstone National Park.

Yellowstone also has abundant wildlife. The Park is home to bison, moose, elk, grizzly bears, black bears, and even wolves. Yellowstone has the largest concentration of free-roaming animals in the contiguous 48 United States.

right: Liberty Cap, Mammoth Hot Springs

below: Minerva Springs and Terrace, Mammoth Hot Springs

Bison and Native Americans

An estimated 30 million bison once roamed the lands of North America, but by the mid-to-late 1800s only a few bison remained, mainly as a result of people killing them for fur, meat, and sport. Some even shot bison from train windows, as the fictional characters Alice and James witnessed, and train companies promoted and advertised such killings as entertainment for travelers. No more than 20 or 30 individual bison could be found in Yellowstone by the early 1900s—and this was considered by many to be the largest wild herd left in North America.

There is evidence that some soldiers—and perhaps civilians, like the fictional character Bloody Knuckles—killed bison as a way to harm Native Americans whose livelihood depended upon the animal. Many Native American groups, especially those living on the Great Plains, considered the bison a sacred animal and relied upon the animal for food and clothing. This contrasted with most settlers' perspectives and ways of life, which were primarily reliant on agriculture.

Bison
Commonly known as buffalo, the animal's scientific name is "bison." A bison can weigh up to 2,000 pounds and sprint 30 miles per hour—three times faster than you can run! Yellowstone is the only place in the world where a wild bison herd has survived continuously since prehistoric times.

Pile of bison skulls waiting to be ground into fertilizer. (circa 1870)

Throughout the mid-to-late 1800s, Native Americans often had their lands taken, were forced onto reservations, pressured to abandon their traditional spiritual and cultural ways of life, and were coerced to use the settlers' agricultural methods. The bison slaughter of the 1800s was only part of this larger complicated relationship between Native Americans and the new settlers. There were many tensions and wars between various Native American groups and new settlers during this time period. One infamous battle even spilled over into Yellowstone National Park in 1877. As the Nez Perce (Ni Mi'i Puu) attempted to escape to Canada to resist being forced onto a reservation, they shot and kidnapped several tourists.

Changing Ideas of Nature

Going on a camping vacation or a peaceful hike in the woods may be common today, but in the 1870s doing such things was considered new and radical. Around that time, some people started to see nature as a spiritual place rather than as a frightening chaos in need of taming and "civilizing."

Henry David Thoreau and Ralph Waldo Emerson, two of the fictional character Mattie's favorite writers, were part of the Romantic and Transcendental movements in American thought, which professed the discovery of God and spirituality within nature. They were intellectual pioneers in helping combine traditional religious teachings with environmental concerns and were staunch proponents of protecting wilderness and animals. In *Adventures in Yellowstone*, Alice was this kind of pioneer as well.

Another widely recognized leader in wilderness preservation of that time was John Muir. Unlike Thoreau and Emerson, Muir was not one to enjoy a leisurely visit to the country and then return

John Muir. (circa 1902)

Some beliefs of the Romantics and Transcendentalists were similar to perspectives of Native American leaders.

> "All men were made brothers. The Earth is the mother of all people, and all people should have equal rights upon it."
>
> —*Chief Joseph*

happily home to a city. The wilderness was his home. As a young man, Muir once walked over 1,000 miles from Indiana to Florida, simply to experience the wonders of the wilderness!

Muir is sometimes referred to as "the father of the national parks" since he was instrumental in creating several of them. Muir used his religious background to write and speak about connections he saw between religion and nature. In early 1866, Muir wrote that the Bible and nature were "two books [which] harmonized beautifully." Muir's greatest contribution to the environmental movement may have been his enduring teaching that nature not be human-centric; meaning, humans should protect nature for the sake of protecting nature regardless of any direct measurable benefit that we may receive.

Around the mid-to-late 1800s, at least two major disagreements began to emerge within the environmental movement itself. First, people like Muir sought to keep civilization out of wilderness areas as much as possible, while others felt that limited human interference with nature was acceptable and perhaps even desirable.

The second major disagreement revolved around the meaning of "environmentalism" and whether or not it should encompass social justice issues. Transcendentalists such as Thoreau believed that humans and nature were interconnected, much like the fictional character James came to believe about the relationship between animals and people. This worldview likely led people like Thoreau to become social activists and speak out against slavery and racism, in addition to being concerned about wilderness protection. On the other hand, other environmentalists of the time focused mostly, if not exclusively, upon land preservation and protecting wild animals, not humanitarian issues. Many of these tensions continue to this very day.

Yellowstone's Nicknames

Yellowstone had many popular nicknames when the Park was created. One popular nickname was "Wonderland," which was based on Lewis Carroll's children's book, Alice's Adventures in Wonderland, *first published in 1865.*

The Diversity of the 1870s

In 1872, there was more racial, ethnic, and religious diversity in the Yellowstone region than is commonly believed. In Bozeman and Gallatin County, the Chinese comprised the largest minority group, followed by blacks and a few Mexican ranch workers. Many Chinese laborers worked under difficult conditions to build the railroad tracks to connect the east and west coasts. Former soldiers and some newly freed blacks also journeyed to the Yellowstone area in search of new beginnings after the Civil War ended in 1865.

Religion and religious language was particularly popular at the time, but many people in the area were more secular, which is why ministers traveled the region to teach gospel. Bozeman was so small in the beginning that for a few years, Christians of varying denominations shared the same church as their worship space. Many towns were also home to minority faiths, such as Jews.

The role of women was beginning to change during this time period. Like the fictional character Mattie, many women were inspired by the political changes occurring in the Wyoming and Utah territories. In 1869, Wyoming became the first United States territory or state to allow women to vote in elections. Political change in the rest of the country was far slower. For example, in Mattie's home state of New York, the feminist leader Susan B. Anthony was arrested in 1872 for voting in an election. It was not until 1920 that women in all states gained the right to vote in federal and state elections, with the passage of the 19th Amendment to the United States Constitution.

Protect It!

As people's concepts of nature evolved, so did their attitudes and actions. Like Alice, James, and Tom in *Adventures in Yellowstone*, many people began to protest against the senseless killing of animals and the destruction of wilderness. Over time, such protestations changed public opinion and eventually persuaded lawmakers to establish and enforce laws designed to protect wildlife and wilderness.

In 1883, hunting was outlawed in Yellowstone, and the United States Army actively began protecting Yellowstone's wildlife against illegal hunting, known as "poaching." Some hunters even began to see the value of giving animals the space to maintain healthy numbers, and gained appreciation for the benefits of preservation. Thanks to these efforts, Yellowstone National Park now has the largest wild bison population in the world, ranging between 3,500 and 4,000 bison.

Profit in Preservation

The Northern Pacific Railroad's original vision of a profitable national park empire held true. Around three million people visit Yellowstone National Park every year to experience its beauty and remarkable wilderness — far more than the 300 tourists that visited the Park in 1872! The United States National Park system, as a whole, now welcomes around 272 million visitors, while creating thousands of jobs and contributing an estimated 10 billion dollars to the national economy every year. As James learned from Aldous Kruthers in the story, bringing people into a protected park is far more profitable than taking apart its features.

Some of Yellowstone National Park's first tourists having lunch in the Upper Geyser Basin. (circa 1880)

Learn More...

The struggle to protect wilderness and wildlife continues in the Yellowstone area. Wolves were recently and controversially reintroduced into the Yellowstone ecology, wildfires started by careless visitors are a constant threat, and animals leaving the boundaries of the Park are at great risk of being killed by hunters. In 2005–2006, the State of Montana helped to kill over 1,000 wild bison that roamed beyond the park's borders.

Many characters and places in our story are based on actual people and places. To learn more about Yellowstone, the history of the time period, and the characters and places in our story, visit our website at www.theecoseekers.com.

The McCartney Hotel where Alice and James stayed was based on an actual hotel built in 1871 by Harry Horr and James McCartney, both real people from Bozeman, Montana. The McCartney Hotel was the only hotel in Yellowstone during that time, and the accommodations were very basic. Guests slept on the floor and were required to bring their own blankets! (circa 1880)

HISTORY NOTES

Adventures in Yellowstone was thoroughly researched in consultation with historians, librarians and educators. This included onsite research at the historical archives of Yellowstone National Park and poring over diaries, newspapers, reports, and other primary sources from the 1800s.

While *The Land of Curiosities* series is historical fiction, great efforts were made to ensure the accuracy of the historical settings, places, and non-fictional characters. The following characters in *Adventures in Yellowstone* were based on actual people: McCartney, Horr, the Bottler brothers, Mr. and Mrs. Story, John and Sophia Guy (of the Guy House), Sam Lewis, Dr. Wright (of the *Bozeman Avant Courier*), Ben Walker, the McDonald boys, and Ferdinand Hayden. References to people like Jim Bridger and President Ulysses S. Grant are also historically based. All other characters were made-up but their experiences are plausible, based on historical evidence.

The following pages include direct quotes and references from primary source documents:
page 1 Gallatin Valley was known in Indian tradition as "The Valley of the Flowers," as stated in Q. K. Club Ladies' Night, Featuring Fred Fielding Willson. **page 2** "Annis and Cooper" was a store advertised in the *Bozeman Avant Courier*, Sept 20, 1871 **page 3** The Guy house is described in excerpts from Mrs. Tracy's speeches and diary. From *Pioneer Woman Tells of Early Home Life,* from the *Bozeman Chronicle*, August 10, 1954: "The hotel where we resided for three weeks until our home was completed was a log structure boarded up on the outside and having a large front porch...Very few conveniences were to be found, the one carpet being in Mrs. Guy's room. The rates were $17.00 per week for room and board." **page 5** Reference to river mosquitos and travel from Homer Thomas, an 8-year-old, in a letter to his grandma. Montana Territory, Dec. 17, 1864: "We had an awful time on the Plains. I don't like that kind of travelling—I would rather take the cars or a steamboat let the old slow oxen go. On the Platte [River], the musquitoes half eat us up, & it was as hot as fire, & mighty dusty." **page 9, 13** The newspaper clip and later quote are direct from the *Bozeman Avant Courier*, Sept. 13, 1871. **page 17** The spelling of Chesnut Saloon was confirmed by Gallatin Valley author Phyllis Smith. Description from Q. K. Club Ladies' Night, Featuring Fred Fielding Willson: "I see on the corner of Bozeman and Main the Chestnut Saloon – a two story building, porch over the sidewalk, a very popular resort. The second floor was given over to all entertainments, dances, concerts, meetings, church socials, suppers and fairs." **page 36** Victoria Woodhull was the first woman to run for President of the United States. She was with the Equal Rights Party and her running mate was Frederick Douglass. **page 38** Alder's Gulch was a prolific mining site in Montana. **page 39** Ranches vs. Farms: "Father took a notion to got down into the Gallatin Valley and take up a ranch. That is what we used to call a farm at home." — Homer Thomas, an 8-year-old, in a letter to his grandma. Montana Territory, Dec. 17, 1864. **page 49, 68** It was common to use religious language to describe Yellowstone ie. "Devil's slide," "Devil's Thumb," "Angel Terrace," "Hell's Half-Acre," were all place-names. See *Between Heaven and Hell: Religious Language in Early Descriptions of Yellowstone.* **page 51-53** Many of the household chores were taken from the *Diary of Reverend William W. Alderson for 1866*: "Finished John's buckskin pants...Cold. Colder. Coldest. Boys stayed home today. Made them some buckskin mittens." **page 55** "The first school building in the county erected with public money was in the winter of 1868 and '69 on the corner of what is now Tracy Avenue and Olive street, a frame structure costing $500, W.J. Beall being architect. This building used for about eight years for school purposes..." from *Early History of Gallatin County* by Mrs. E. Lena Houston. **page 57** Many people who went to the hot springs sought to heal venereal diseases. **page 57-59** The Bannock walking through town from the *Bozeman Avant Courier,* Sept. 20 1871: "A whole tribe of Bannack Indians, number we should judge by the length of time required in passing through town, about one thousand, Chief Tendoy in command, arrived in Bozeman on Sunday, and are now encamped near town...some gaily bedecked with red flannels, red blankets and numerous other fancy trapping, while occasionally could be see a [woman] with three of four of her progeny all mounted upon one dilapidated kiyus...

in a few days they will proceed to the Yellowstone and Snake river regions where they will spend the winter hunting." **page 80** "Poop Valley!" was a quote borrowed from a modern kid during an on-site Expedition Yellowstone! tour. **page 98** The description of a hotel was from a diary. **page 99** "Sam [Lewis] was a very, very fine colored gentleman who, with his son, played for many of the dances, he the harp and his son the banjo. 'Fan me with your fan dear and call me a nice young Man.'" From Q. K. Club Ladies' Night, Featuring Fred Fielding Willson. **page 102** "McCartney built it over an oblong, human-sized hole fed by nearby spring water through a hollow trough." This specific description was taken from a diary. **page 103** The Toxic Cave was from a diary. **page 157** The biography of Bloody Knuckles and the Long Coat Gang was invented, as was the newspaper blurb about the missing girl.

The terms *Native American*, *American-Indian*, *Indian*, and specific tribe names, refer to the people (and the descendents of the people) who inhabited what is presently the United States prior to European discovery of the Americas. There are currently different opinions among scholars and even Native tribes themselves as to how to properly refer to this group.

PHOTO CREDITS

front cover Hot Springs of Gardner River: Courtesy National Park Service, Yellowstone National Park, William H Jackson; 1871. Mammoth Hot Springs with Langford on formation; k# 64,107; William H Jackson; 1872. **page 166 (and back cover)** The magnificent New Virginia Canyon Road and Virginia Cascades, Yellowstone National Park. Copyrighted 1905 by T. W. Ingersoll. Courtesy Library of Congress.
page 167 fishing: Courtesy National Park Service, Yellowstone National Park, YELL 129235, H.B. Calfee, photo taken between 1873 and 1884. **(and back cover)** Native Americans: Courtesy National Park Service, Yellowstone National Park, YELL 37742, William Henry Jackson, photo taken in 1871. NOTE: This photo was not taken in Yellowstone, but likely somewhere in Idaho. The so-called Sheepeater tribe is the only known Native American nation to have resided year-round within what became Yellowstone National Park, but by 1871 the tribe relocated to the Shoshone Wind River Reservation. Guard House: Courtesy National Park Service, Yellowstone National Park, YELL 30351. This photo of the old guard house on officer's row was taken in 1917. The guard house was built by the U.S. Army in 1891 to protect the park from poachers and other 'shady characters'. **(and back cover)** Giant Geyser: Courtesy National Park Service, Yellowstone National Park, YELL 129260, H.B. Calfee photo taken in the early 1880s. Some of Yellowstone's first tourists gathered around the so-called Giant Geyser. **page 171 (and back cover)** hunters: Courtesy National Park Service, Yellowstone National Park, YELL 697, F. Jay Haynes. **page 172** Old Faithful: Old Faithful Geyser in the winter; Upper Geyser Basin; Photographer unknown; 1964. Courtesy National Park Service. Old Faithful Geyser; Upper Geyser Basin; George Marler; No date. **page 173** Mammoth Hot Springs: Minerva Springs & Terrace; Mammoth Hot Springs; Photographer unknown; 1965. Courtesy National Park Service. Liberty Cap: Liberty Cap; Mammoth Hot Springs; Photographer unknown; 1963. Courtesy National Park Service. **page 174** bison: Courtesy National Park Service. Bison at Soda Butte in winter, The Thunderer & Mt. Norris in background; Jim Peaco; January 1997. **page 175** bison skulls: Courtesy Burton Historical Collection, Detroit Public Library, circa 1870. **page 176** John Muir: Courtesy Library of Congress. **page 178** Alice: Illustration by John Tenniel, in public domain. **page 181 (and back cover)** picnic: Courtesy National Park Service, Yellowstone National Park, YELL 129272, H.B. Calfee, Photo taken between 1873–1884.
page 183 McCartney Hotel: Courtesy National Park Service, Yellowstone National Park, YELL 676, F. Jay Haynes.

PRAISE AND AWARDS FOR *THE LAND OF CURIOSITIES* BOOK 2

LOST IN YELLOWSTONE

"A captivating adventure story that inspires a sense of wonder."
RICHARD LOUV
Author, Last Child in the Woods

"Use this book to foster a preservation ethic in the most important generation — the next generation."
SCOT MCELVEEN
Former President, Association of National Park Rangers www.anpr.org

"Captures the thrill of good literature as a vehicle for that enticement, excitement, and curiosity of our national treasures by the next generation."
BRIAN A. DAY
Executive Director, North American Association for Environmental Education

"A brilliant job of weaving history with exciting adventure. This book inspires young people to be the change they want to see."
MIKE MEASE
Co-Founder, Buffalo Field Campaign

INDEPENDENT PUBLISHER BOOK AWARD
Juvenile and Young Adult Fiction (GOLD)

NAUTILUS BOOK AWARD
Teen Fiction (SILVER)

Additional awards include **MOONBEAM CHILDREN'S BOOK AWARD** (SILVER), and **MOM'S CHOICE AWARDS®** (SILVER) for best young adult historical fiction.

ADVANCE PRAISE FOR *THE LAND OF CURIOSITIES* BOOK 3

RED EYE OF THE BUFFALO

"This series inspires a connection among young readers with that great American Idea, National Parks. These stories are engaging, and bring the adventures to life of young people who care deeply about their natural world."
ERICA JOSTAD
President, Association of National Park Rangers

ACKNOWLEDGEMENTS

We would like to thank:
Yellowstone National Park and the National Park Service,
Lee Whittlesey (Yellowstone National Park Historian),
Yellowstone National Park Heritage & Research Center,
the Yellowstone Gateway Museum, Expedition: Yellowstone!,
the Bozeman Public Library, the Montana Historical Society,
our talented illustrators and their agents,
Rev. Sally Bingham for her faithful encouragement,
Susan Manilow, Kevin J. Coyle at NWF, Phil Gutis at the NRDC,
Coila Ash at ForestEthics, Della Schweiger, Sally Shepard,
Kathleen Rooney and everyone in Senator Durbin's office,
Betsy Watrey, Rebecca Humrich,
Jenna Lanterman and The Calhoun School Middle School Book Club,
Anya Aboud, Ethan Gunnlaugsson, Laura Neil, Mark Neil, Daniel Fischel,
and our editors Janice Phelps, Molly Dumbleton, Rachel Billow,
and especially Sandra Winicur, and our educational editor Christy Kingham.

A special thank you to:
Elijah Hayes Neil for being born and inspiring our adventure,
Sylvia Neil for her guidance with the manuscript and tour of Yellowstone,
Daniel Frohling of Loeb & Loeb LLP for his wise and generous counsel,
Keith Glantz for designing our logo and website,
and, most importantly, Paula Winicur for her tireless efforts
since the very beginning of our journey.

*This book is dedicated to our grandmother, Ruth,
and to Sandra Winicur. We miss you.*

DEANNA NEIL is an award-winning author, playwright, singer, educator, and journalist. She has been featured in *USA Today, ABC News,* and *Time Magazine for Kids* named her a 2008 "Hero for the Planet." Deanna currently lives in Los Angeles, and frequently visits Yellowstone National Park and Grand Teton National Park.

Conceived by **DAVID NEIL**, the EcoSeekers was founded in 2006 by the brother-sister duo of David and Deanna to entertain and inspire the next generation of environmentalists. The company was awarded "best first book" (silver) by the Independent Publishers Association, and has been featured on *Good Morning America Now.*

David is a longtime champion of children's literacy, and is a recipient of the Celebrate Literacy Award from the International Reading Association. David is a real estate executive in New York City and the proud father of three boys. He considers The EcoSeekers his fourth child.

David and Deanna in Alaska, August 2001